W9-CBO-642

ELLEN LOWELL—trapped on an emotional roller coaster, she switches from one man to another to try to slow down.

DAVID STEWART—he believed he had found his worst enemy—until, to his surprise, he falls in love with her.

PENNY HUGHES—even after her parents try to stop her, she will not stop loving the wild, hot-tempered Jeff.

JIM LOWELL—his climb to social prominence makes him think he can get away with anything, including an affair the whole town knows about.

———————

Story Editor **Mary Ann Cooper** is America's foremost soap opera expert. She writes the nationally syndicated column, *Speaking of Soaps*, is a major contributor to leading soap opera magazines, and has appeared as a guest on numerous radio and television talk shows.

Writer **Bob Bancroft** is a native of Vermont. Besides writing for such diverse publications as the *Boston Globe* and *Soap Opera Digest*, he has acted in numerous TV commercials and soap operas. He currently resides in a beachside enclave near Los Angeles.

Dear Friend,

In 1956, AS THE WORLD TURNS premiered, promising to transport viewers to new heights of drama. Certainly keeping that promise, the show remains one of the most popular soaps on the air. That's why I was delighted to help put together this paperback book series based on AS THE WORLD TURNS.

With a team of the finest romance writers in the marketplace today and the use of original scripts and stories, Pioneer Communications Network, Inc., has created an exciting new genre of books.

Book 1, *Magic of Love*, establishes the Stewart, Lowell, and Hughes families. Thrill to the early courtship of David and Ellen Stewart as they find happiness despite fate's cruel blows against them. Book 2, *Ruling Passions*, looks at the next generation of Hughes family members when Bob meets the captivating and ambitious Lisa.

For Soaps & Serials Books,

Mary Ann Cooper

Mary Ann Cooper

P.S. Pioneer Communications Network, Inc., has many more soap opera books in the works. Write to me at Pioneer, 825 Brook Street, Rocky Hill, CT 06067, and I'll tell you all about our latest paperback series.

AS THE WORLD TURNS

Magic of Love

&Soaps™ &Serials

PIONEER COMMUNICATIONS NETWORK, INC.

Acknowledgments

The publisher wishes to express his appreciation to Joshua M. Brand of Taft Merchandising Group, who has held fast to his belief in this project and assisted throughout the development of these books. Special thanks also to Susan Carnes, John Valenti, Ken Fitts, and Ted Busch of Procter and Gamble Productions, Inc.

Magic of Love

AS THE WORLD TURNS paperback novels are published and distributed by Pioneer Communications Network, Inc.

SOAPS & SERIALS™ is a trademark of Pioneer Communications Network, Inc.

ISBN: 0-916217-41-8

Printed in the United States of America

10 9 8 7 6 5 4 3 2 1

Magic of
Love

Chapter One
A Surprise Trip

"Good morning."

"Good morning, dear."

"Coffee, Chris?"

Without waiting for an answer, Nancy poured a cup for him, then a careful half cup for herself. They had been married nearly twenty years and that first cup of coffee never tasted quite right to Nancy Hughes unless she had poured one for her husband first.

Poor man, he's certainly the worse for wear, she noted with concern. Being up half the night preparing a brief for today's court appearance hadn't done much for his appearance either. She slid the morning edition of the *Oakdale Gazette* a few inches closer to his left hand, then moved the cream and sugar within easy reach of his right. He's been driving himself too hard lately, she fretted, and Jim, who's supposed to be helping him on the case, is no use at all. And now for Jim to go gallivanting off to that convention in Buffalo—it was just plain irresponsible, that's what it was, especially at a busy time like this.

Instantly she felt a twinge of guilt. Though she often questioned their values in life, she was nonetheless very fond of the wealthy Lowells, especially Jim's wife Claire. Now there was another disturbing thought. Poor Claire. What was going on with her? Sad and angry, vulnerable yet hardened, she seemed resigned to some fate Nancy could only guess at. The Lowells, the most fashionable couple in the country club set, seemed so perfect on the surface. Still, some question lingered in Nancy's mind, some as yet unformed suspicion.

There, now, she chided herself, don't meddle in other people's affairs. Your own family needs your attention, particularly that groggy man staring blankly at the front page of the paper. How soon will it be, she wondered, before Chris can share his workload with one of the boys? With any luck it'll be Don—he's a good deal older than Bobby, and he certainly has that lawyer's way with words. But that's years away, she reminded herself. All things will come in good time, she thought, sighing, as she padded to the stove to scramble some eggs.

"Nancy, did you see this?"

Of course she hadn't. She liked to give Chris a fresh paper each morning, as sort of an everyday affirmation of his position as head of the family. Then, when he had left for the office and the rest of their family had gone their separate ways, she would settle down with a nice full cup of coffee and take her own sweet time absorbing the day's news before she began her housework.

"Read it to me, dear. I've got to watch the toast." She checked for a reaction but saw none. Nothing registers yet, she thought with amusement.

The toast was a running joke in the Hughes household. For all her skill in the kitchen, somehow she could never make toast to her husband's specifications. She relished the familiarity of the routine, mostly because she suspected that Chris' gentle complaints were all part of a playful game designed to remind her how important she was. With satisfaction she compared her domestic skills to those of her sister-in-law, Edith, and chuckled aloud. Then she stopped immediately as she saw the expression on Chris' face.

In one swift motion she pulled the frying pan from the stove and turned the eggs onto the plate. Breakfast in hand, she moved quickly to her husband's shoulder. "What on earth," she asked, "has you so—" then stopped abruptly as she saw what had caught Chris' eye.

Jim Lowell woke up with a start. Where am I? Why am I here? His eyes darted around the darkened room in a frantic search for familiar objects. He flung back the damp and knotted sheet and struggled to extricate himself. Free at last, he lay back down on the pillow and inspected the room once again.

In the pre-dawn gloom he saw what he hoped he'd never see, the realization of his worst and most private fears. It couldn't have happened, yet somehow it had. What should he do now?

The last agonizing days of his life flashed before his eyes, and he saw himself as some sort of B-movie patsy, in mockery of his actual standing as a pillar of the community. Uncontrollable rage welled up through every fiber of his being, and its force frightened him through and through. He fought an urge to run, to escape everything. Quickly he made a last-ditch effort to re-assert control. Don't panic, he ordered himself, then listened helplessly as his mind echoed back Panic, panic, panic.

"No!"

He leaped from the bed, shocked by the sound of his own voice. His feet hit the floor with a thud, and suddenly he realized where he was. He was back—he was home. Relief flooded his body. His pulse slowed, and he checked the other bed to be sure Claire was still sleeping. He wriggled his toes into the carpet as if to assure himself that he was indeed in his own room, his own house, his own life. Shivering less from the cold than from an effort to rid himself of that intrusive nightmare, he slipped on his robe and headed for the door.

Then, all at once, without warning, his heart pounded wildly. The panic had been so close, so palpable, and the very thought of it brought him to the brink of terror once again. I can't live like this, he told himself, and again the echo came back. Live like this, live like this, live like this. That insistent voice, so moralistic: it would drive him mad. He hurried for the stairs, hoping against hope that the voice would stay in the bedroom. Before he could stop himself, he asked, do I deserve this? Yet again came the awful answer, I deserve this. I deserve this. I deserve this.

He grasped the railing for support. What a way to wake up! He prayed that the rest of the morning would go better, then, with a rueful grin, he asked himself what right he had to make any requests from God. He'd solve this dilemma himself. It was quite a predicament, but at least he had one advantage: no one suspected. Not Claire, thank God, or Ellen, that sweet innocent girl, or Chris, or Nancy. There had to be a way out, and he'd find it, if it was the last thing he did.

Immediately he regretted his choice of words. It would be the first thing he did, and he'd do it today, this very morning. Resolution strengthened him, and he took a deep breath and exhaled slowly. Perhaps this would work out, after all, and he might even be able to turn the situation to his advantage. He strode purposefully through the living room and pulled open the French doors which led to the terrace. Ah, the intoxicating smell of spring, he thought, such a reaffirmation of life. It gave him just the sense of renewal he so desperately needed.

Instinctively he turned to gaze at the northern sky, the way he had as a small boy. The unfulfilled longings of his youth pulsed through him, and their familiarity both comforted and reminded him how far he had strayed. But all would be well, he vowed firmly, and there was a fine life waiting for him. He could find his path to happiness—it was right in front of him, right here in Oakdale. He only had to extricate himself from . . .

"What are those lights, dear? The aurora borealis?" His wife had materialized soundlessly at his side.

"No, Claire, it's Chicago." He regretted the sarcasm in his voice as soon as he heard it, but she had interrupted his fantasy. He slid his arm around her shoulder and held her close to him. He would have to work very hard to keep his resolution.

"Can't I fix you some breakfast? Please, dear?"

She was begging to be needed, and it irritated him. This was going to be much more difficult than he had thought. "I'm late," he said abruptly, and turned on his heel, leaving her alone on the terrace staring blankly into the sky. Daybreak swallowed up the waning stars and brought light into the heavens. Yet Claire Lowell saw only a dark and meaningless void.

"Last one in is an old maid!"

"Oh, no, I'm not!"

"Yes, you are! You don't even have a date for the prom yet."

"Only because I can't decide who to say yes to."

The excited, high-pitched shrieks brought Nancy out of her reverie with such a jolt that she dropped the whole bag of clothespins to the ground. She peered between the rows of sheets and towels, across the back yard, through the breezeway and out onto the front lawn. Was school out already? She'd been so preoccupied all day that she must have lost track of the time.

"I'll be right in, girls," she called, but they were already out of sight, no doubt rummaging through the refrigerator, she was sure. She pulled the remaining clothes off the line and hastily folded them. Today she was particularly glad Penny was home, and she was pleased she'd brought Ellen with her. Their innocuous chatter was certain to chase away any unpleasant thoughts.

She parked the laundry basket in the pantry and paused for a moment in the doorway to gaze fondly at her eldest daughter. It hardly seemed seventeen years since that wondrous day Chris had rushed her to Oakdale Memorial.

Actually, it hadn't seemed so wonderful then, she recalled. She had been terribly frightened, not so much by the excruciating pain she was sure would come, but by the awesome responsibilities of impending motherhood. Would she measure up? Her simple girlhood, spent in several tiny towns in the Midwest, seemed inadequate preparation for the complexities of raising a family in the suburbs of Chicago. Even then, Oakdale was losing its bucolic charm, and Nancy remembered being concerned that life here would soon begin to move faster than she could handle. It all seemed so ludicrous now that she, Nancy Hughes, might fail at being a mother, but at the time it had been a deeply troubling worry. Only Chris' solid support and quiet strength had restored her confidence.

And now before her sat Penny, the first of her four children, and the one upon whom Nancy placed all of her most precious hopes and dreams. A woman loves all her children equally, but no matter how much she tries not to, she reserves a special place in her heart for her firstborn, Nancy believed. And at the moment

Penny was occupying that spot with grand and youthful style.

"But, Ellen, did you *see* him?" she bubbled gaily, the fabric of her skirt a whirl of blue as she pirouetted across the linoleum. "I think he's the dreamiest!"

Nancy wondered how the language of teenagers could change so much from year to year, yet always remain the same. Surely she hadn't been so frivolous when she was Penny's age, she thought, then realized that it was only because she hadn't had the opportunity.

"Jeff doesn't exactly have the best reputation in school, you know," her chum countered primly.

At times Ellen was an uncomfortably accurate reflection of her parents' less admirable qualities, thought Nancy. "Who's Jeff, dear? I haven't heard you mention him before." She disguised her motherly curiosity with an offhand tone.

"Just the handsomest boy in the whole senior class, that's who. And I don't care who likes him and who doesn't." She flounced to the refrigerator, plucked out an apple, and took a large, juicy bite.

"Oh, Penny, you always try to sound so rebellious," snorted Ellen. "Gimme an apple too."

"Try and make me." With a mischievous grin, Penny tucked an apple behind her back.

Eyes sparkling, Ellen made a grab for it. "Hand it over, or I'll . . ." Triumphantly she snatched the fruit from her friend. Consumed by giggles, the girls gathered up their school books and papers and dashed out of the room.

"Is that going to be enough nourishment for

you children?" Nancy asked with amused tolerance, but they were already thundering up the stairs to the room Penny shared with Susan.

Teenagers are such peculiar creatures, she thought. One minute they're acting like kids, and then the next minute they're all grown up.

"Am I interrupting?"

Nancy turned around, smiling. "Dad." The gentle voice belonged to Chris' father, the children's beloved Grandpa Hughes, and she wished she could have the benefit of his counsel right now. Instead she asked, "What can I get for you?"

"Just some of your time, dear. You've been a million miles away all day—and I can tell you're worried about something."

"Oh, it's nothing, really. At least I hope—I mean, I think it's nothing." Nancy was doing a poor job of convincing herself, and her father-in-law didn't look as if he would buy it either. "Anyway, it doesn't concern you or the family or anyone you care about."

Nancy never snapped at Grandpa, but the strain of telling an outright lie had made her unexpectedly angry. She looked around for refuge and suddenly remembered the laundry. She brought the basket into the kitchen and carefully refolded the last few items.

"Um, Dad, I'm really not myself today, though that's hardly a good excuse for talking to you like that." Her apology brought a tolerant and understanding smile to Grandpa's face, but Nancy didn't feel any better for it. Why couldn't she and Chris just tell him the truth? Chris wanted to. But it wasn't their secret, and besides they weren't even sure it was true. Or, at least, Nancy wasn't sure. And this time she was holding off passing judgment.

She picked up the pile of fresh linens, sniffed it with satisfaction, and made for the stairs. The girls wouldn't be as inquisitive as Grandpa. They were so much more interested in boys, school, clothes, hair that they didn't have time for adult problems. As she walked past Chris' den, she looked in, and in her mind's eye she saw a tiny Penny rolling around on the floor, merrily tumbling in her father's strong arms. The picture was as clear and vivid to her as if it had happened only yesterday. And now that innocent baby was about to graduate from high school. It hardly seemed possible. Nancy's only regret, and it was a painful one, was that her own parents couldn't be there for such a milestone.

She quickly filed away the sadness her realization produced, took a deep breath, and headed up the stairs. Life is a continuum, and that knowledge brought her comfort. Her father had given her inner strength and an unshakeable belief in God's power, and in that way he remained a part of her forever. From her mother she'd learned a joyous, zestful philosophy of life, tempered by the practical common sense that was part of her now. Yet of all her mother's gifts, the most priceless was her capacity for unconditional love. It was the one quality she was determined to pass on to Penny, so that Penny's children could be loved as much as Penny was, and as much as Nancy had been by her parents.

Ellen's voice reverberated down the stairwell. "Well, she sure doesn't dress the way I'd ever care to. And her behavior!" She tsk-tsked in just the way Nancy found most annoying, especially in one so young. "I certainly wouldn't want all of Oakdale talking about me behind my back, and she doesn't even seem to notice."

"It's all a question of what's important to people." Nancy swallowed with pride as she heard her daughter stand up for a person's right to individuality. "Personally, I like her. I admire her for not always doing exactly what other people expect of her. She believes in herself, and I hope I grow up just like her."

Who was this mysterious person? Clearly it was not a classmate. Nancy paused midway on the stairs, curious about this controversial person.

"Well," Ellen retorted, "of course you like her, but you don't need to stick up for her all the time. My mother can't stand her, and neither can I. I'd just die if she were my aunt."

Edith! Nancy took in her breath in one sharp gulp. Frankly, now she wasn't quite so thrilled at Penny's passionate defense of nonconformity. Edith thought she was too fascinating, too independent, to be bothered with the tiresome conventions of Oakdale, but to Nancy she was selfish, self-absorbed, self-obsessed. She simply thought of no one but herself, and she made no secret of the fact that she considered Nancy an interloper in the Hughes family. Nonetheless, Nancy was cordial with her and never failed to include her in family functions. But having Edith serve as a role model for impressionable Penny was another matter indeed, and Nancy didn't know how to put a stop to it. The problem had been building for quite some time, and she had simply preferred to ignore it. Edith was a strong adversary—Nancy knew that only too well. Furthermore, she did have a right to live her life the way she saw fit, no matter what Nancy or the rest of Oakdale thought about it.

"If you'd seen her yesterday," Ellen continued, "you wouldn't be quite so proud of her. She was acting downright peculiar."

"What are you talking about? Aunt Edith is out of town until the weekend. I know 'cause she told me herself. She went to Chicago to look for some summer clothes. Heaven knows, there's nothing in this town that's suitable for her."

Penny was right. Edith had gone out of town on a shopping trip, or at least she said she was going to go, Nancy recalled with growing anxiety.

"I saw her at the train station yesterday, when Mummy and I went to pick up Daddy. He was so exhausted from all those meetings in Buffalo. I'd never seen him like that. Mummy and I were helping him with his suitcases when I saw your aunt Edith get off the same car as Daddy, except from the rear door. At first I didn't think it was her. For one thing, she was wearing a big floppy hat so you couldn't see her face, and then, when she saw us, she headed the other way. Now you know as well as I do that she and Daddy are friends, and she acted like she didn't even see him. Except—and here's the odd thing—when she thought Mummy and I weren't looking, I saw her give Daddy this really strange look, like . . . well, I don't know what it was like."

In a flash Nancy realized what that glance had

signified, and she dreaded facing it. It was all too obvious now. When Chris had shown her the picture in the paper this morning, her first impulse was to think that it was all a mistake. That just couldn't have been Edith in the background of that photo from the lawyers' convention. After all, Edith was in Chicago, buying a new wardrobe so she'd be chic in the summer heat in Oakdale. That's what she had told everyone, and after all, what could have been more plausible? It really had been a great cover story, and Nancy had bought it. She'd defended her sister so many times, saying that Edith was an essentially good, though misguided woman. Now she felt betrayed. Edith had been lying to everyone but, most of all, to her brother, Chris. How could she have done such a thing? Edith had not gone on a shopping spree. She hadn't been in Chicago at all. She had been in Buffalo with another woman's husband, and the very idea of it made Nancy sick. And to think that this was the woman her Penny idolized. Well, not for long, she concluded grimly.

"She must have just changed trains or something and come back early." Penny's explanation was a trifle glib. Had she suspected all along?

Nancy cleared her throat and stepped into her daughter's room. Trying to sound casual, she said, "Here, honey, will you put these away for me?" and handed her a stack of towels. "I've got to start dinner. Ellen, would you like to stay?"

"No, thank you, Mrs Hughes. I want to be home tonight. My father has been gone all week, and then last night he had to go out for something or other, so he promised that tonight he would spend some time with me."

Nancy's heart ached for her. And her anger rose and rose until she felt she would burst. So many innocent people were being hurt. Ellen, poor Claire, Chris, and Grandpa. But Nancy couldn't bring herself to meddle. This was one time she would keep herself out of it. Definitely, positively, she would keep her mouth completely shut. Maybe if she repeated that to herself often enough, she might believe it.

Chapter Two
The Betrayal

She took one final look in the mirror, made a last-minute adjustment to her hair, then jumped up from her dressing table and hurried for the door. As she strode through the living room, she paused briefly to admire her reflection in the full-length mirror which stood between the buffet and the chaise. A fine figure of a woman, she complimented herself, deserving far greater rewards than life had given her up till now. She drew herself up, threw her head back and tossed her lustrous brown locks. Too dazzling, she thought. I'm just too intense. He likes his women quiet and unassuming, mousy even, she thought with disdain. Well, I can conceal only so much. Either he loves me the way I am, or else I'll . . . she decided she would think about that later.

She moved to the door and struck a pose which she hoped was the right combination of subtle feminine appeal and not-so-subtle sensuality. She leaned forward to peer through the peephole, just to make sure it was him. But there was no one there. She yanked the door open, stuck her head out, and looked up and down the empty hallway. I've done it again, she said to herself. That's the fourth time this afternoon I've done this. She slammed the door then held her ear to it to see if any of her neighbors had heard.

"Truly," she said aloud, "I am becoming quite vexed." That sounded properly cultured, she thought. A lady of her refinement should maintain her image even in so tiresome a situation. When Jim had called her that morning, he had said he was coming right over, and his voice had had a ring of urgency, she remembered. Then he had called and said he wouldn't be able to come until later that afternoon, but that he wanted very much to talk to her. Talk? What was there to talk about? She didn't want to talk. Last night they had certainly done no talking. What could have happened between last night and this morning that they should talk about? Edith Hughes, she said to herself, was entitled to more than idle conversation, and she would see to it that she got it.

It didn't matter that she'd only recently succeeded in making Jim a part of her life. Now that he was, she had absolutely no intention of letting him go. Those last few days they had spent together had sealed their relationship, as far as she was concerned. He had made certain promises deep in the night, there in the hotel room in Buffalo, and she was determined that his obligation would not fade in the clear light of day in Oakdale. She distractedly fingered the bouquet of gladioli he had brought her last night. Glads—so brilliant, so showy, she thought. So unlike Jim, yet so very right for Edith.

So where was he? This was really becoming too much to bear. She certainly wasn't about to call his office, and not just because her brother might very well be there. In fact, she didn't really care that much what Chris knew about them. He'd had his chance to give her what she needed in life, and he'd chosen not to, so now she was just going to have to go after her heart's desires in her own way. And if Chris didn't like how she went about it, well, that was just too bad, now wasn't it?

Perhaps she would change her dress. That should kill some time. Anyway, now that it was nearly evening, her light blue floral print was no longer appropriate. What should she choose? She moved to her closet and opened the door. Her theory about housecleaning was that it should be confined to those areas of the apartment that people were likely to see, and her closet was not one of those. Her burgundy dress was lying in a heap on the floor, underneath a pair of shoes and a blouse, so there went that idea. Without enthusiasm she began to shuffle through the garments that were still on hangers. Jim's imminent visit was losing its appeal with each passing moment.

Well, she decided with resignation, I've got to choose something, and I might as well do it now. The grey cocktail dress was a trifle formal, and she didn't want to look as if she considered his visit a special occasion. Wait, she thought, that simple navy sheath I got last month will be just perfect. She slipped it on and moved immediately to her dressing table. Pearls would be an exquisite finishing touch, but should it be a single strand or a double? She was starting to feel a little bit less anxious now. In fact she began to hope that Jim would be delayed just a few minutes longer.

She settled herself luxuriantly on her stool, as if she had all the time on earth. Her dressing table was her favorite spot in the whole world. She loved the graceful curve of the mirror, the elegant gleam of the glass top, the opulent excess of the rows and rows of bottles and tiny jars that lined the top and the one little shelf. But, most of all, she loved the pink ruffled cover. She laughed aloud to think of it, that she, Edith Hughes, loved pink ruffles, but it was true. To her they seemed to symbolize everything she desired— beauty and charm, both for herself and her surroundings, as well as affluence, security and, most of all, love. In fact, it was only when she sat here at her table, with those ruffles brushing softly against her knees, that she felt truly and completely loved.

Jim stood in the hallway for what seemed to him like an eternity, his finger poised over the doorbell. How on earth was he going to handle this? It had seemed so simple this morning. All he had to do was to be straightforward with her, to explain how their affair would affect everyone and why they had to end it. If only he had come over first thing, right after he had awakened, when the memory of his dream was still so fresh and painful. Then the shock of thinking he'd awakened in Edith's room instead of his own would have pushed him into putting a stop to this foolishness once and for all. Because that's what it was, pure and simple. It was foolish for a married man to carry on with another woman when he had no intention of doing "the right thing" by her. And in a situation like this, what was the right thing anyway? He had a wife he loved very deeply, and a daughter he adored, and if they ever found out about this, it would break their hearts. Poor Claire was fragile enough already, and Ellen . . . He refused even to think about what it would do to that innocent teenager if she ever found out. And find out she would, unless he not only broke off his relationship with Edith, but also convinced her to keep their liaison a secret in the process.

He'd already learned about Edith's disregard for other people's feelings, and he did not want another lesson like that. With trepidation he'd agreed she could accompany him to the convention, but he'd made her promise to keep out of sight. She did not do that. When she showed up unannounced at the closing night dinner, he thought he'd have a heart attack right then and there. But she laughed off his concern, blithely assuring him that no one noticed and, even if anyone did, no one cared.

"These are the 1950's," she proclaimed brightly, "not the Dark Ages! Now, Jim, let's forget about everyone else. Let's live life for the moment and never look back. Let's just think about us and what we can have together, and society be damned!"

Somehow those hundreds of miles away, her words touched a chord deep within him. The world was changing and Jim wanted to change along with it. He was over forty and he'd been with the same woman for nearly half his life. He felt that he was missing something and he didn't even know what. Life held many mysteries and he had investigated so few of them.

After a staid and proper boyhood in Oakdale, he had gone away to college and then law school at the same university. It was there, in his undergraduate years, that he had met Claire. They had married right after graduation. Together they had moved back to his home town and had started a family almost immediately, and Jim had gone to work in the law practice owned by his father. His whole life, it seemed, had been planned out for him—everything had been somehow predestined. There'd been no surprises—he had never before done anything unpredictable. He had been completely devoted to doing what was expected of him, and now he felt trapped.

In the beginning, Claire had been very appealing, like a helpless little puppy. She had depended on him for everything and had looked up to him as if he were her father. He had been her whole world, and it had made him feel strong and good and worthwhile. Then Ellen was born. It had been a difficult pregnancy but an even more difficult delivery. For a while there, it was touch and go, but Claire pulled through eventually. It was a few months later that he started to notice the change in her. She became moody, withdrawn, and often obsessed with Ellen.

Everything had to be just right for that child, and though Jim loved the baby more than he could ever say, he still resented how completely Claire focused on her.

Despite the growing coldness at home, it was years before he even looked at another woman. In fact, his affair with Edith was the only indiscretion in his marriage. And now, that one mistake was threatening to shake his life to its very foundations.

Unfortunately, the choice was not as clear-cut as it had seemed at dawn, for Edith Hughes was a fascinating woman, the opposite of what he had known for twenty years. She appeared to need no one and to be completely sure of her own self-worth. She really did practice what she preached—she charted her own path in life and didn't care whether anyone else approved or not.

Claire was very different. Vulnerable, quick to feel pain, she cared passionately what her friends and neighbors thought, and Jim realized that the anguish this might cause her would be almost more than she could bear. And as for Ellen, although she was a teenager, to him she was still only a baby, with an unformed sense of morality. A revelation like this could destroy her, as well. Quite frankly he had to decide whether or not Edith was worth it.

A typical lawyer's approach, he thought wryly, to place all the pros on one side, and all the cons on the other, and then to see which one tipped the scales. With relief tinged with regret, he could see what his true feelings were.

He felt his strength returning. He knew what he must do. Jim Lowell had always taken the righteous and noble path, and tonight would be no exception. He pressed the doorbell firmly until he was sure the melodic chimes sounded throughout the apartment.

Claire Lowell picked up the phone on the first ring. Surely it was Jim, just calling to say he'd be home momentarily. It was really getting quite late. "Yes, dear," she said. "Dinner's almost ready. Will you be here soon?"

"Mummy, it's me!"

Suddenly Claire realized that Ellen wasn't home from Penny's yet, and she hadn't even noticed. She hadn't been able to concentrate on anything but Jim all day. When he woke up this morning, his mood had been so disturbing, so strange and so full of foreboding somehow. Then he had dashed out of the house without eating breakfast or reading the paper. And she hadn't heard from him since.

"Is Daddy home? He promised me he'd spend time with me tonight and I can't wait! When will he be there? Didn't he tell you?"

"No, honey, he didn't. He's not here yet, but I'm sure he's on his way." Claire wanted to get this conversation over with as soon as possible. Ellen's incessant questions were getting on her nerves. She just couldn't cope with worrying over Jim and trying to assure her daughter that everything was all right at the same time. "I'll call you when he gets here."

"Mummy, Mrs. Hughes asked me to stay for dinner and I said no because I thought Daddy would be home but now since he's not, can I please?"

"Can you what?"

"Stay here for dinner. Please, Mummy."

"Of course. Fine. Call me later. Tomorrow's Saturday, so you don't need to be in early. Goodbye, dear." She hung up the phone quickly, so that Ellen wouldn't have a chance to say any more. She just wanted to be alone.

This house is so empty, she thought, and so eerily quiet. She walked slowly into the kitchen and looked around. Everything was just as she had left it that morning—newspaper still folded on the table and, next to it, coffee cups, napkins, silverware. She still hadn't eaten breakfast, or lunch, for that matter. She hadn't really eaten for days, not more than a few bites anyway. It was just too much effort. Idly she picked up the paper and opened it to the front page and stood there, rooted to the floor, not wanting to believe what she saw.

Ah, finally. And wouldn't you know it, just when I was beginning to enjoy being by myself. Edith ran a practiced hand over her hair, arranging it just so, inspected her makeup carefully, and made for the door once again. This time it wasn't a false alarm, and she didn't know if that made her happy or not.

"Jim Lowell. What a surprise!" The offhand tone she affected was as much to benefit her neighbors as it was to put Jim in his place. She closed the door gracefully and automatically modulated her voice to that husky contralto she knew he found so alluring. "I've missed you desperately. Where have you been all day?"

Already he felt himself weakening and

imagined himself melting into her arms. To be desired so totally by such a woman—it gave him that heady feeling he hadn't experienced since the first time Claire had given herself to him. "Working, Edith," he said, mustering up all his reserves of self-control. "I've had a lot to catch up on, a lot of responsibilities."

"Surely you have time for me," she purred. "Life isn't all drudgery." She moved to the buffet and set up two glasses. "I know just what you need to perk you up. The weekend is coming, and I've got the perfect way to kick it off."

He heard the ice clink against the glass, saw the bourbon splash down over the cubes, watched as Edith then held both drinks aloft in her beautifully manicured hands. Yet he said nothing. Languidly she settled into the sofa and held out his drink to him. He sat down beside her.

"Was there something you wanted to talk to me about?"

Her question caught him off guard. Not that it had slipped his mind. He had simply forgotten that he had forewarned her. He took a long pensive sip before speaking. "Us."

She knew what was coming. He was so duty-bound. Not only was he the kind of man who would do right by his wife, but he would also be honest and above-board with his mistress. It would almost be cute and endearing if it wasn't happening to her. She had to do something about this right away.

"I know, dear. I've wanted to talk about us too." Her mind was racing. What would she say next? What was it that he needed to hear? She'd just have to take a stab at it. "Jim, you know I care for you a great deal, and there isn't anything I wouldn't do for you. But I feel a little guilty. I feel I've led you on and drawn you into a relationship you're not ready for." She glanced up at him, demurely she hoped, and saw an almost imperceptible look of relief on his face. She forged ahead confidently.

"If I'm not what you want, or there's something about me that you can't accept," she said, "then I want you to know that I'll understand. I won't do anything to stand in the way of your happiness." Her voice cracked and she dabbed at an imaginary tear. This is really too corny for words, she thought, but it seems to be working.

Jim sat up just a little straighter, then reached over and held her. He had never seen Edith quite like this, so delicate and so selfless. Her body quivered slightly in his arms. Soon she would be racked by sobs—he could feel it coming. "Edith," he begged, "please don't cry. Just try to listen to what I have to say."

She sniffed, looked at him with eyes that were bigger and more soulful than he'd remembered, and snuggled closer to him. "It's Claire," he continued. "My place is with her, and no matter how much I love you, I can't abandon her."

He had never said I love you before, and she pounced on it. "Oh, Jim, I love you too, and to see you torn like this . . . well, it hurts me more than I can say. Jim, I promise you I won't make any demands. Just stay with me a little while longer please." She reached up and drew him closer, then slowly, inexorably, she guided him to her. He didn't resist.

Jim turned the key in the lock, opened the door, and flicked on the front hall light. Had Claire and Ellen gone out? Perhaps they'd decided to take in a movie. It couldn't be so late that they'd gone to bed. He left his hat and coat on the banister, his briefcase beside it, and headed for the kitchen. He was famished, and he hoped Claire had left him something in the refrigerator.

He paused in mid-step. Something was wrong. He didn't think he'd ever heard the house so deathly quiet. The air outside was still—no breeze rustled the curtains. No creaks of the floorboards did he hear, no whirr of appliances, no snatches of music drifting down from Ellen's room at the far end of the upstairs hallway. He tiptoed, afraid to disturb the silence.

At the doorway to the front parlor he stopped. Finally, a sound broke the hush. Tick-tock, tick-tock, tick-tock—it was the grandfather clock, unnaturally loud as it echoed across the room. All at once he remembered he had been holding his breath, and he sighed long and deeply. This day had seen him in both the depths of despair and the heights of ecstacy. He was exhausted, worn out through and through. Too tired to turn on the light, he sank down on the couch in the darkened room, closed his eyes, and began to drift away to that pleasurable place somewhere between wakefulness and slumber.

"Jim."

He lurched forward and switched on the table lamp, and there, sitting in the small, straight-backed chair next to the window seat, was Claire. She must have seen him come up the driveway, must have heard him enter the house. And there she was, so quiet and ladylike, her hands folded primly on her lap, her face an unreadable mask. *The Oakdale Gazette* lay neatly at her feet.

"Jim." Her voice was quiet, unnaturally calm, yet with a strength he had never before heard. "What is the meaning of this?"

"I'm just late, dear. I've had an awful lot of catching up to do. Those few days in Buffalo really set me back at the office."

"No." There could be no mistaking her intensity. "No! I'm not asking why you're late. I want you to explain something to me. Tell me about this, Jim." She held up the newspaper.

He dreaded looking. Somewhere inside himself he knew what he would see, and he knew what it meant. He felt sharp twinges of pain up and down his arm and all through his shoulder. The tension was taking its toll. He had been right all along. Edith Hughes would only bring him misery. He could see his life crumbling in front of him, and he was powerless to stop it.

The photograph swam before his eyes. Damn that woman, he cursed. How could she have done this to him? "Claire," he said, "I love you, though I don't expect you to believe me at this particular moment, and I'm going to tell you the truth about Edith and me. I've got to get it off my chest."

"I don't want the truth! I don't want the details. I want you to stop. I want you to promise me you'll never see her again. I want you to make this up to me, Jim Lowell!" Very agitated, she got up from her chair. "I want you to take me away from Oakdale, far, far away, and I want you to make me forget that any of this ever happened. I've given you my life, and now I want you to give me yours. You've betrayed me—you've stuck a knife in my back." She was shrieking now. "You've humiliated me in front of everyone. How will I ever face my friends? And Nancy? What about Nancy? I can never let her see me again as long as I live!" She paced up and down the rug, oblivious to Jim's confusion and growing horror.

He stared at her dumbly, her ranting and raving rained down on him and produced no effect at all. He was in shock. He had always known that Claire was inclined to be nervous, but he had never let himself think that she could become seriously unbalanced.

"I'm divorcing you! You're no better than an animal. You have no feelings, no morals, nothing. You don't deserve me. You deserve a woman from the gutter," she flung over her shoulder as she rushed out of the room, "and I hope you rot in hell!"

He watched in despair as she disappeared up the stairs—then he turned to gaze at the face of the clock. Damn that thing! It stopped for nothing, just kept ticking along. He felt a sudden urge to smash it and was looking around for an implement when out of the corner of his eye he noticed someone moving stealthily through the hallway. He wheeled around, half-expecting a renewed attack from Claire.

"Daddy." Poor Ellen was as white as a sheet.

He reached out for her, his flesh and blood, to comfort her, but she looked at him with loathing.

"Don't touch me! Don't you ever touch me, ever again!" Then she too was gone.

Chapter Three
The Conflict

"It's my favorite holiday, Mrs. Hughes. I like it even better than Christmas." Jeff Baker stood in the corner of the kitchen, surveying the frantic last-minute preparations. Nancy was basting the turkey just one last time, Grandpa was putting the finishing touches on his famous cranberry sauce and Penny and Susan were rushing around, taking care of all the side dishes. Actually, Penny was doing most of the work, but somehow she was manipulating her little sister into believing that the candied yams and the creamed peas and onions were completely Susan's creations.

It was Nancy's favorite holiday too, the one she looked forward to all year long, and the one that always created the most satisfying memories. She was determined that this year would be no different.

"Jeff, bring us some water too." That was Don calling from the back yard, where he and his father were tossing around a football. It was curious to Nancy that brisk fall air seemed to make all men think of sports, even when the rest of the year didn't produce such a reaction. She poured a couple of glasses of water and handed them to Jeff.

"Thank you, Mrs. Hughes."

"You're welcome, Jeff." He was always so polite and respectful to her, yet he made her uneasy. It wasn't his good looks, though heaven knows he was extremely blessed in that area. Tall, reed-thin but sinewy, with a fine-featured face capped by a thatch of unruly brown hair, he cut quite a figure in Oakdale. All the young women desired him, but Penny was the one who'd captured his heart. That made Nancy quite nervous, and she didn't know why.

His family background was hardly conventional, but Nancy couldn't bring herself to hold that against him. He lived with his father on the outskirts of town in a run-down trailer surrounded by cars, most of which were up on blocks in various stages of repair and disrepair. His mother lived and worked in the center of town, but she had always found her son too much to handle, so she had left most of his upbringing to her ex-husband.

Although Nancy felt sorry for him in a way, still she didn't quite trust him with her Penny. For one thing, he was wild and reckless. This she knew for a fact. One Friday night she and Chris had been coming home from an evening with the Lowells, and they had been nearly run off the road by a couple of cars hot-rodding down the highway. Nancy had recognized one of the drivers as Jeff, and although he later apologized profusely, she never completely forgot the incident. She tried to attribute it to youthful high spirits and extremely poor judgment.

She was even more worried about Jeff having an explosive temper. She'd never witnessed it personally, but she'd heard that he sometimes reacted violently when his racing buddies challenged him.

All this gave Nancy intense anxiety, and she felt it during most of her waking hours. Penny was now a sophomore in college, and though she was living at home, she was too old for the kind of discipline Nancy and Chris had used when she was younger. Nancy had tried reasoning with her, and she and Chris often joined forces to try to talk some sense into her, but Penny remained adamant. She loved Jeff and was determined to go on seeing him. Nothing anyone said could dissuade her.

Nancy's latest approach was to accept Jeff, to invite him over, to include him in family gatherings. In short, she did nothing to encourage Penny's rebellion. This wasn't as hard as she had initially thought it would be, for she was quite fond of Jeff. He really was a very appealing young man. But she couldn't wipe that one thought out of her mind, that vaguely apprehensive feeling perhaps only a mother can sense, that a relationship with Jeff would end unhappily for her daughter.

But today was no time for such thoughts. Thanksgiving was a day for just that, giving thanks, and Nancy intended that this would be a holiday to remember. "Are we all set, Grandpa?

Should I call in the boys to wash up? Oh, but before I do that, I want to make a quick phone call." This year, in particular, she wanted to be sure to wish Claire a pleasant, enjoyable holiday with her family, and she wanted to do it before it was too late. And soon it would be.

She headed for the phone in the hall and crossed paths with Jeff in the living room. "Oh, Jeff, are you sure you can't stay? Penny would love it, and of course you know you're always welcome here." She would have felt hypocritical, but she really did like him, she reminded herself.

"Thank you, Mrs. Hughes. I would like to stay, but I should be with my parents, don't you think? Did I tell you? We're all having dinner together."

He took such boyish pleasure at the thought of seeing his mother and father at the same table that Nancy found it easy to forgive him anything. And anyone who regarded family as being so important couldn't be all bad. She patted his arm. "That's wonderful, Jeff. We'll see you soon."

She dialed the Lowell residence and soon had Claire on the line. They exchanged the customary greetings, inquired about the health of husbands and children, yet neither one of them could bring themselves to mention the one person on both their minds. It galled them both that after years of friendship, countless confidences, and endless sharing back and forth, the one thing that really bound them together was Edith. Neither one had invited Edith into their lives because they had wanted to—they only tolerated her because they had to.

But this Thanksgiving Claire had something special to celebrate: Jim had assured her that Edith was out of his life once and for all. This time she believed him. Ever since that fateful day a year-and-a-half ago when he had finally confirmed her suspicions, he had tried to rid himself of his obsession with Edith. Now it seemed that at last he had. The toll it had taken had been terrible, not only on Claire but also on Jim. He had aged so much in the last year, and his struggle to regain his youth was a dismal failure. Claire now felt protective of him very much as he had been of her in the first years of their marriage.

"I'm just thankful," she was telling Nancy, "that we're together this year. And for all the unhappiness I've endured, I have learned one important lesson. When I thought I'd lost my Jim, my first worry was what everyone would think of me. But now that I have him back, I can tell you that he's going to be my focus, not my club meetings or lunches or parties. So you see, all this does have a bright side."

The doorbell rang and Nancy cut her off hastily. It was wonderful to hear Claire so hopeful, and she prayed nothing would spoil her newfound happiness.

She moved to the door and opened it wide. "Edith, you're just in time."

Dinner had been a grand success, as always, and now Nancy was hurrying to finish her cleaning so that she could join the family in the living room. Usually Chris and a couple of the children helped her, but Edith had insisted that they all

join her in looking through old photo albums.
Nancy could hear snatches of conversation
drifting in.

"Here, Susan, look. Here you are getting ready
for first grade, your very first day of school. And
look at that bow in your hair. It's almost as big as
you are," her sister teased.

"Where are all the pictures of you, Penny? I see
plenty of Susan, but almost none of you." That of
course was Edith. She'd always taken exception
to Nancy's handling of Susan, the baby of the
family, but this was hardly the time to mention
it.

"Don, who is that girl you're with, and what
on earth is she wearing?" Penny adroitly changed
the topic. His reply was inaudible, but it brought
laughter from the whole family. Nancy decided
to leave aside the rest of her work until later. This
sounded too good to miss.

Edith was seated in the big easy chair, the one
by the fireplace that Chris always sat in. The
children were sprawled at her feet, and Chris and
his father occupied the sofa.

"Oh, come in and join us, Nancy dear. Surely
you can spend a few minutes without your
apron." Edith was making the most of her
position at the center of the group. "Goodness,
where will you sit? This room is so cramped." She
turned to her brother. "Chris, you simply must
remodel. I don't know how poor Nancy tolerates
it."

"It's never seemed small to me before." Nancy
restrained herself with an effort. She was not
about to let her sister-in-law goad her into an
ugly exchange of insults. Not today of all days.

"You know what you must look at—the new salon at the country club. You've seen it, haven't you? It's just been redone and it's marvelous, the very latest thing." Edith prattled on as if Nancy hadn't said a word. "Well, of course you'd know all about it if you'd joined the country club when everyone wanted you to. Chris, I can't understand why you let Nancy talk you out of it."

"She did no such . . ."

Edith laughed in that playful yet thoroughly calculating way she had whenever she wanted to make her brother angry. "I know. You never do anything you don't want to do, and you never let Nancy make decisions for you. Such an appealing picture of domestic bliss, don't you think?"

"Edith." Grandpa's tone was low and ominous. "This is not your home. This is Nancy's and Chris' home, and I would appreciate it if you'd respect that fact."

"What did I say? What did I say wrong?" Edith's affectation of outraged innocence was almost believable.

"Never mind, Edith, it's not important. Children, it's time for you younger two to go upstairs," Nancy said, trying to hide her displeasure from her children. "Penny, Don, will you take Bobby and Susan to bed? I'm going to get the coffee."

An uncomfortable silence settled over the room. No one spoke until Nancy returned minutes later with a trayful of cups and a pot of freshly brewed coffee. Chris jumped up to help her, and Grandpa cleared space on the table.

Edith stretched lazily in the big armchair. "I'll have sugar and double cream," she announced, then added as an afterthought, "please."

No one moved for a moment. Then Chris got up and put another log on the fireplace. Unhurried and cool, he poked the embers, then replaced the screen.

Nancy poured coffee first for her father-in-law, then for her husband, and last for herself. She settled back on the sofa and leaned against Chris' shoulder. "Edith," she said sweetly, "please help yourself to some coffee. That is, if you'd like some."

"I apologize from the bottom of my heart if my manners are not up to your standards, Nancy," Edith said with careful deliberation, "but I haven't had the advantages you've enjoyed. My life, you should know by now, has not been easy."

Chris jumped at the bait. "Not only does that have nothing to do with my wife, but also it's a poor excuse for your selfish outlook on life. Dad and Mom gave us both a good start in life, and we should be grateful for it."

"We didn't both get exactly the same treatment," she snapped, "and you should allow yourself to admit that fact, Chris. You got a college education, without which, I would hasten to remind you, you would still be back on that dreadful farm where we grew up."

This was more than Grandpa could bear. His happiest memories came from that farm, and it didn't matter that those years were full of poverty and hardship. What he recalled most of all was the deep love. "Your mother and I . . ." he began, faltering as he spoke.

"Don't talk to me about Mother. That farm ruined her, and I don't want to hear another word about it. That winter you hurt your back, do you remember what she did? Chris of course was away at college, too occupied with his own life to help us out. Mother milked the cows and took care of everything in the barn, and then she insisted on shoveling the coal into the furnace all by herself. She was too stubborn to hire anyone to help her, and neither of you ever did anything about it. You know, that's the way I remember her, heading out to the barn in the afternoon, wearing one of those awful sweaters with the holes in the elbows, and I could never invite my friends over. I was so afraid they'd see her. And I vowed that when I grew up, I wouldn't be anything like her."

"Well, Edith," Grandpa said drily, "you have certainly succeeded in that. You're nothing like your mother, and though it pains me deeply to say it, I'm glad she didn't live long enough to see how you've turned out. You're my only daughter, and I love you, but I don't understand you. I don't know where your anger and resentment come from, or why you feel the world owes you a living. I know I must accept my share of responsibility for the kind of person you are, but I did my best, and the rest is up to you. Look at your brother—he grew up in the same house, with the same parents—look at what he's done with his life."

"You put him through college! How many times do I have to say that? You squandered your life savings to provide your son with a college education, and there was nothing left for me.

You know, it was always that way. I was always second-best. Nothing was too good for Chris, but as for Edith, well, she can just take care of herself. Let me tell you, I intend to. I intend to do just that and I hope you're prepared."

Penny and Don came down the stairs and looked in shock at their aunt. Nancy motioned them both back upstairs, but neither one moved. Incidents like this were extremely rare in the Hughes household, and they were fascinated.

"I was supposed to get my college education after Chris had gotten started with his law practice." She continued her diatribe. "But oh, no, those promises were forgotten just as soon as he had that diploma in his hand and virtuous Nancy on his arm. The money he made belonged to me, instead of to Nancy and his damned children. I'll never forgive any of you for that. Most of all, I'll never forgive you, Nancy. You saw a good thing when you met my brother. You made sure he didn't get away, and you didn't care who you hurt. And you have the nerve to act like you're better than I am!"

"Edith!" Grandpa spoke with force and clarity. "It is time for you to leave. But before you do, I want to hear you tell your brother you're sorry, and more important, I want you to tell Nancy you didn't mean what you said."

"No! I'm not done yet." Edith went on with almost maniacal intensity. "I can see that none of you cares anything about me. All you think about is yourselves and your own petty lives. From now on I intend to go after what I want, just like all of you have, and I intend to get it. I don't care what anyone thinks or what anyone says. I'm looking out for myself, since none of you have any interest in my welfare." With that, she plucked her coat from the rack and stalked out.

Several weeks later Nancy received a phone call. She was all the way upstairs in the boys' bedroom when the call came—she didn't reach the phone until the seventh ring.

"Hello?" she said tentatively, sure that the caller would have hung up. "Hello? Is anyone there?"

She heard only silence, then suddenly, a sob, then several. "Who is it? Who is this? Claire? Claire, is this you?"

The sobs quieted slowly, and when she finally spoke, Claire's voice was small and weary. "Nancy . . . oh, Nancy, please help me."

Chapter Four
Shock Waves

It was the coldest winter to hit Oakdale in a decade. The Arctic winds blew down over Lake Michigan with a fury unmatched in anyone's memory. All over town, people wrapped themselves in extra scarves and wore warmer hats. They all prayed for an early spring.

Only the children seemed immune to the winter's severity. This would be the year they'd look back on when they were thirty-five and remember that the snowdrifts had been ten feet deep, and they'd built caves, castles, and snowmen bigger than they'd ever made before. This would be the year the skating pond had stayed frozen from before Christmas until the first week in March. But for Penny Hughes, this would be the year she had put the love of her parents to its ultimate test.

When a break in the weather finally came, it was brief but tantalizing. For a few days, the mercury rose as high as forty-five degrees. Gentle breezes blew, and the sun peeked over the treetops to spread its warmth to the bushes and plants below. Penny and Nancy stood with the front door open, marvelling at the sudden change in weather.

"Don't you dare tell your father I've left the door open like this," Nancy giggled. "You know how he is about wasting heat."

"Yes, mother," Penny replied automatically, "I know." She turned and went back to the kitchen and sat down.

Nancy followed her. "I wish, dear," she said, "that there was something I could do to make you feel better. Your father and I are very worried about you."

"Don't you think you have done quite enough, Mother?"

"We thought long and hard, dear, before we . . ."

"You thought about yourselves and what you wanted, and not about me and what I want. It's my life and, despite what you think, I am old enough to make my own decisions. I love Jeff, and we belong together, and nothing you or Dad can do will ever change that. I just don't know if I can forgive you, that's all. What you forced me to do . . . oh, I can't even talk about it." Choking with sobs, she rushed out of the room.

She needs to be alone, Nancy told herself, and besides, she does have a point. It is her life. But they are just so young, too young for the responsibilities of marriage, and Chris and I just couldn't let a moment of impetuosity ruin her life. That's why we did what we did. Our motives were pure. When she's a parent, she'll understand how we feel and why we took matters into our own hands.

It all came back to her, that rush of conflicting emotions that had welled up in her that day Jeff and Penny had walked in the kitchen door arm in arm. "We have an announcement," Penny had said shyly. "You tell her, Jeff."

Nancy had called Chris immediately. "The children eloped!" she'd cried. "Our little Penny got married. Oh, Chris, what shall we do?"

With Chris' legal expertise, they devised a way to have the marriage annulled, and then together they broke the news to Penny and Jeff. You're too young, too immature, and we want our daughter to have a chance to finish her college education first, they said. "Please understand," Nancy begged, "we're doing this for your own good."

Months passed, yet Penny still did not accept the situation. She continued to see Jeff, at first behind her parents' backs, and later, quite openly and defiantly, in front of their faces. Nancy and Chris had never seen her quite like this. It was almost as if the trauma had given birth to a new Penny, a stronger, more forthright woman who believed in herself with total faith. But what caused Nancy such deep anguish was that this personality switched to a passive, dependent, morose Penny, who seemed incapable of doing anything but bursting into tears. It was because of this that the Hugheses hadn't forbidden their daughter to see Jeff, nor had they barred him from their home. They were so concerned with Penny's deteriorating mental condition that they agreed not to do anything that might add to her anguish.

They would have preferred that Penny break off with Jeff completely, and though they knew this would be best in the long run, for the time being they did nothing to prevent Jeff and Penny from seeing each other. Better Penny should see him with our knowledge than that she should be doing it behind our backs, they rationalized, little knowing that until they had agreed the two could spend time together, they had been sneaking around Oakdale going from one clandestine meeting to the next.

It took all of Nancy's strength to refrain from speaking her mind to her daughter, for she believed in her heart that Penny was rushing headlong into disaster. But Chris insisted that they keep the avenues of communication open, so Nancy used restraint. It wasn't easy.

"Dear," she said, "may I come in?" She waited doubtfully at Penny's door.

"Of course, come right in. I want to tell you something." Her tears had dried, her sniffles stopped, and in their place was a cool, even gaze that implied strength and self-possession. "Jeff and I are going out tonight. He's picking me up in a few minutes, and I don't know when we'll be back. I don't want you to wait up for us."

"All right, dear, but if it's going to be unusually late, your father and I would prefer it if you would give us a call. The roads are still pretty icy, and though I'm sure Jeff is a skillful driver, I wouldn't want us to spend the evening worrying." Nancy chose her words carefully. Experience had shown her that arguing with Penny when she was like this only encouraged further defiance. Settling for partial control was better than having none at all, she supposed.

"Well, Mother, that's up to you. I'm going out with Jeff, and how you choose to deal with it is your own business."

Nancy was on the verge of breaking her promise to Chris and giving Penny one quick lesson in the responsibilities and duties of parenthood, but she was cut off by the blare of Jeff's horn. She parted the curtains, and sure enough, there was Jeff sitting in his old jalopy out on the street. Dusk was beginning to fall, and a few lone snow flurries blew up and flickered in the beam of his headlights. "Please be careful," she murmured and turned to say goodbye, but she was talking to an empty room. Seconds later she heard the front door slam, and the noise of the jalopy shattered the quiet of the peaceful neighborhood street. Then they were gone.

"Mrs. Lowell?"

"Yes, this is she." Claire didn't recognize the caller's voice. "May I help you?"

"We have the results of your test ready."

"Excuse me? To what test are you referring?" Claire was becoming puzzled. "Who is this, please?"

The woman on the other end of the phone chuckled, "Oh, I'm sorry. I thought you knew. Surely you were expecting our call. This is Dr. Grayson's office. Congratulations." Claire was silent, at a loss for words.

"Your test results," the voice continued, "came back today. The reading is positive. Are you sitting down? You're pregnant, Mrs. Lowell."

"I'm . . . I'm sorry, but there must be, I mean, there has . . ." she stammered. "I'm sure this is all a mistake." What kind of cruel joke was this, Claire thought. Was this another of Edith's machinations, yet another scheme to drive a wedge between Claire and Jim? It just didn't make any sense. For one thing, Claire could not be expecting a baby—that was completely out of the question. She and Jim had been a couple in name only for quite some time now. Most nights he slept in the den, that is, when he came home at all. Their marriage was on the shakiest ground it had ever been, thanks to Edith. Claire recalled the Thanksgiving just over a year ago, when she'd told Nancy that Jim was finally free of Edith once and for all. But she realized later that their reconciliation was a sham. The following year had been twelve months of manipulation and plotting from Edith, and it had brought the desired effect. Jim and Claire were on the brink of divorce.

And now this. What could it mean? Had Edith arranged some way to rub salt in her wounds? Just what was going on?

"Mrs Lowell? Mrs. Lowell? Are you still there?"

"Yes, I'm here." Claire was slowly returning to reality. It had to be some sort of silly error. "But I'm convinced there is some mistake. I haven't taken any medical tests of any kind, not for years."

The woman hesitated. "This is Mrs. Lowell, isn't it? Mrs. Ellen Lowell?"

Penny whirled around the tiny dance floor, secure in Jeff's strong arms. The jukebox held a selection of all the current favorites, but her special song was "Walkin' After Midnight." It wasn't the latest thing or the newest hit record, but it was hers and Jeff's. To them, it told the story of their love, and how they'd searched and found each other once again, and they felt that when Patsy Cline sang, she warbled those words for them alone. The only other song of hers they liked any better was "Sweet Dreams," and that was because the mournful tune gave them a chance to dance slowly, to move as one in the safety of their own private world.

And now, here it was. As the heartbreaking song began, Penny and Jeff were transported in an instant. She gazed deeply into his limpid gray eyes and saw there the man of her dreams, with whom she planned to spend the rest of her life. As he held her, he felt strong and manly—the petite young woman in his arms needed him and loved him. He vowed to protect her always and leaned down to whisper in her ear, "I love you forever and ever."

So oblivious were they to anyone else that they didn't even look up when a scruffy-looking man strode in and demanded, "Where's Jeff Baker? I've got a score to settle with him."

Roughly, the man pushed aside the other couple on the dance floor then stood before Penny and Jeff. "I've been looking for you, and now that I've found you . . ." The rest of his unspoken threat was communicated by the vicious gleam in his eyes.

"Who is this? Jeff, what does he want?" Penny asked fearfully.

"Al James. I beat him once in a race, and he's

never forgotten it." Jeff's reply was brusque, and he didn't shift his eyes from his adversary.

"You broke the code, Baker! The code says you give me a re-match, and you refused. You said no, you were done with racing. I say you're chicken. I say you were chicken to race me then and you're chicken to fight me now. Isn't that right, Baker?" he taunted.

"Please, Jeff, let's get out of here. Just turn your back and leave," Penny pleaded, dreading the violent force of Jeff's temper.

"That's right," Al needled. "Just run away from me. Hide behind your girlfriend's skirts. What a man!"

Jeff turned, squared his shoulders, and faced him head on. His eyes glinted bright. The cords in his neck were stretched taut. "I'm ready, James"

"No! Jeff, no!" screamed Penny as she lunged between the two men. Momentarily distracted, Jeff sidestepped her and slammed into the jukebox. Before he could regain his balance, Al caught him first with a quick left jab then a hard right that felled him and ended the fight almost before it had begun.

"There's more where that came from, and don't forget it. If you ever cross my path again, I'll see you get more of the same." Al James hitched up his pants and swaggered out.

Jeff painfully struggled to his feet and wiped a trickle of blood from his mouth. The instant the reality of what had happened hit him, his rage came forth in a relentless surge. "I'll get you for this, Al James, if it's the last thing I do. You won't live to brag about this, I warn you, because the next time I see you, I'll kill you!" he hurled at the back of his departing foe.

"Jeff, you don't mean that," Penny cried in horror.

"I do. I swear I do. I mean it more than I've ever meant anything in my life." He was quaking with anger. "Come on. Let's get out of here."

Penny grabbed her coat and purse and followed him out into the night. When she reached the jalopy, he was gunning the engine with impatience.

"Hurry up, will you?" he snarled. "I've got something to take care of."

Ellen Lowell scurried up the walk as fast as her legs would carry her. What a night for her car to refuse to start. She'd left it in the parking lot near the college library and had called for a cab. But in Oakdale taxicabs were used mostly by senior citizens to take their groceries home from the supermarket and were operated at a speed appropriate to that task. By the time Ellen was picked up on campus she was already delayed over an hour, and by the time she got home she was nearly two hours late.

Just before she got to the front door she felt the nausea rise then, just as quickly, subside. This is supposed to happen only in the morning, she could not stop herself from thinking. No, no, it's just nerves, she willed herself to believe. It will stop as soon as I hear from Dr. Grayson, she consoled herself, as she opened the front door and shook the snowflakes off her clothes.

"Ellen, you're so pale. Is something wrong?" Claire was standing at the foot of the stairs, looking a little sick herself.

Ellen gritted her teeth and pushed the queasiness far back down inside herself. "I've just had a bad day, and my car wouldn't start, and I'm cold and tired and coming down with the flu." She managed a weak smile. "Other than that I'm fine."

"You must sit down immediately and let me bring you something hot to drink, some tea perhaps," Claire said as she darted into the kitchen.

Ellen's uneasiness increased. Her mother seemed unusually solicitous tonight. She hoped it was her imagination. She lay back on the sofa and breathed deeply trying to think of other things. But one overriding question kept reasserting itself. She had to know. Would Dr. Grayson still be in his office? She made an effort to get up, but suddenly she was too tired to move. Her mind was too full of conflicting thoughts to produce any rational answers. She was more confused than she had ever been in her life.

"Dear, something very peculiar happened today." Claire spoke softly and without emotion as she set down the tea. "Dr. Grayson's office called with the most inexplicable message. His nurse said you had taken some tests . . . Would you like to talk to me about it?"

"Oh, Mummy." Ellen burst into tears. "I wanted to tell you. Honest I did, but I didn't know how. I'm in a terrible jam and I don't know what to do, and I need you to help me. It's true—I'm pregnant. I'm having a baby, my own little baby is inside me, and I don't know what to do."

Claire stroked her hair and murmured, "I'll help you. Whatever you decide, I'll stand by you." Such sentiments are far more worthy of Nancy Hughes than of socialite Claire Lowell, she mocked herself. Perhaps I'm changing in ways I'm not even aware of, she thought. Then she asked Ellen gently, "Have you thought about what you want?"

"I know what I don't want. I don't want a baby!" Ellen fairly shrieked. "I can't have a baby. I just can't."

"It's a fact of life, dear. You're pregnant. What happens next is that you have a baby," Claire replied, calmer about the situation than she ever would have predicted. But then she had had several hours longer than her daughter to digest the information.

"Mummy, what do I do? What now?" Ellen wailed.

"Well, dear, the first thing we're going to have to do is to tell your father. I'll be there with you, or I'll even tell him for you, if you'd prefer, but he does have a right to know. Despite everything that has gone on between us, he is still my husband and your father. He is essentially a good man, and we must be honest with him. Then your father will talk to the young man and convince him to stand up to his responsibilities."

Ellen's sobs redoubled in intensity. "Never! It'll never work. Mom, you just don't know what I've done. I was so lonely, so unhappy, and I wanted to do anything besides be here with you and Daddy. Please, I'm not blaming you. You'll hate me when I tell you. He can't marry me. He'll never marry me. Mom, he's already married!"

This was the blow that sent Claire reeling. The problem was far more enormous than she had thought that afternoon. A simple pregnancy, a hurried and hush-hush wedding — that all sounded so easy compared to this dilemma. There would be no nice way out of this, and Claire was glad for only one thing. She was thankful that her agonizing difficulties with Jim had taught her that she must follow the dictates of her own conscience rather than the standards set up by society.

"Who is he, Ellen?"

Ellen's reply was muffled, but at last she got the name out. "Tim Cole, Dr. Tim Cole. We've been seeing each other for months now, but he'll never ask for a divorce. Now that this has happened, he'll never look at me again. I just know it. Oh, Mom, I've ruined my life. I've been such a fool. I'll pay for this for the rest of my life, I'm sure I will. I don't deserve to be this baby's mother, and that will be my punishment."

In an instant Claire comprehended the meaning of her daughter's words, and she knew that she too would pay a bitter price. Tucked safely away in her daughter's womb was her first grandchild, a tiny speck of life about to become a human soul that Claire would never have the opportunity to know. She realized this and she wept.

Penny was inconsolable. The evening with Jeff had been such a fiasco, such a shattering turn of events. And his reaction to it had been downright scary. She had insisted that he take her home immediately, and that he go somewhere and cool off. He had dropped her off without a word.

She couldn't ask her parents for advice, not now, not after what she'd said this afternoon. So she turned to her brother.

Don had just started college that fall, and to Penny he showed every indication of growing up to be a fine young man. That is, if he could ever make up his mind what he wanted out of life. He was forever questioning himself, unsure if he should be a lawyer or not, or if he was interested in this girl or that girl. Though he wasn't sure about how to deal with his own life, he showed a deep understanding of the problems of others.

So Penny was pleased to arrive home to find that Chris and Nancy had retired early, and Don was parked at the kitchen table surrounded by textbooks. The moment he looked up, he knew something was wrong.

"What's up, sis? You and your honey have a fight?"

"Much worse than that." Penny fought to hold back the tears. "Jeff got into an awful brawl tonight," she began, then told him the whole horrifying story. When she got to the part where Jeff threatened Al, she tried to make light of it, but to Don it was apparent that this was the crux of the matter. Penny was frantic from fear that he would retaliate, and that the situation would get completely out of hand.

"I'm sure Jeff has too much sense for that," Don assured her, "but if you're really worried, I'll hop in the car and see if I can find him."

"Don, would you? I won't sleep a wink tonight if I think Jeff is out there aiming for revenge. If you had seen the look on his face or heard what he said, you would know exactly how I feel. He was so out-of-control, and I'm very frightened. When he got hit, it touched some nerve inside him, and he was like a madman. What should I do, Don?" The more Penny talked about it, the more upset she became.

Don spoke rapidly but surely. "If you think there's some reason to think Jeff is about to do something serious, then we should call the police and not waste any time about it. But if you think this is something that will blow over in time, then we should just sit here and wait for him to call. Those are our choices."

"I don't know what Jeff will do. I wish I could read his mind, but I can't. The one thing I do know is that I don't want to be alone. Not now. Please stay with me and talk to me. That's the only thing that will help." A tear formed in the corner of her eye, then another and another. Soon she was weeping softly, almost imperceptibly.

Don helped her into the living room and laid her down on the sofa, cradling her in his arms. "There, there, it's not so bad as all that. You've had quite a shock, that's all. But by tomorrow this will all be behind you." He patted her arm and held her, and before he knew it, she was sleeping like a baby.

The phone rang shrilly, punctuating the silence with its insistent jangle. The first three rings were part of Penny's dream, but the fourth brought her up off the sofa like a shot. Who could be calling at this hour? Fearfully she picked up the receiver and breathed, "Hello."

"Penny, I'm so glad you answered. I need you." Jeff sounded strange and faraway. "Please say you'll help me."

"Jeff, of course I will. But did you have to call me so late? It's after midnight. Let's talk about it in the morning," Penny whispered quietly, too weary to be irritated at him.

"No, Penny, don't hang up!" His urgency reached through the telephone wires and gripped her. "I can only make one call."

"Why? What's happened?" She was fully awake in an instant.

"It's a long story. I hope you're ready for this," he said.

It seemed as if she stood there for an eternity, motionless, offering only an occasional uhn-huhn or mn-hmn. She twisted the phone cord around her wrist, then untangled it. At one point, she said, "Really?" then held the phone away from her ear while he yelled. "I didn't mean that," she apologized, then listened intently as his narration continued.

When he was done, she hung up the phone and raced upstairs to her parents' bedroom.

"Dad! Wake up!" she commanded as she shook his shoulder. "It's me, Penny. Wake up."

Chris sat up straight and wiped the sleep from his eyes. Nancy reached over and snapped on the bedside light. "What's wrong?" they asked in unison.

The words tumbled out in a torrent. "I've made a terrible, terrible mistake. It's Jeff. I never should have left him alone tonight. This is all my fault. If only I'd been with him, this never would have happened. And now his life is ruined forever."

Nancy put her arms tightly around her daughter's shoulder, and Chris said, "Start at the beginning and tell us what you're talking about."

Penny took a breath then told her parents about going dancing with Jeff, their rude interruption, and how the evening had ended. With a catch in her voice, she recalled how she'd demanded he take her home. Then she tried to describe the phone call that had just come, but her emotions got the better of her, and she couldn't go on. Nancy handed her a tissue and Penny began again.

"Jeff called me from police headquarters. He told me that the police discovered Al James's body in the parking lot near where we were tonight. After they made some inquiries, they picked up Jeff for questioning. I guess he didn't say the right things, because . . ." Penny stopped. She didn't want to hear what she knew she must say.

She gulped then bravely turned to face her father. "Dad, I want you to help him. Jeff is being charged with murder!"

Chapter Five
Life and Death

Betty Stewart couldn't believe her good fortune. Barely a month ago she was unwilling to go on living. Her husband, David, was contemplating sending her away for a "rest" in a nice secure residential home in upstate New York. Though he was one of Oakdale's finest doctors, he was unable to cope with the behavior she exhibited. They were both at the end of their ropes.

Then a miracle happened. Their prayers were answered, and now Betty thought she must be the happiest woman on earth.

When she had married Dr. David Stewart, she had taken her wedding vows to heart. "For richer, for poorer, in sickness and in health," they had both repeated, never dreaming how prophetic those words would be. In the early years of their marriage, they had struggled mightily against mounting financial pressures. Finally when David's practice became more secure, they were able to pay off all the money they had borrowed to put him through medical school, and they started building a life of their own.

That's when Paul had been born. The news that she was pregnant had come as a shock to both of them, but they'd immediately accepted it with all the joy expected of new parents. When problems with Betty's health had surfaced in her fifth month, they'd sought out the best medical advice available in Oakdale. But it had been useless. The delivery had been traumatic and her recovery difficult.

David had been forced to hire a full-time nurse to look after Betty and to take care of the newborn baby boy. Eventually Betty had gained strength, and she'd been able to take over many of the household tasks she'd abandoned. Paul had grown into a sturdy toddler and, slowly, Betty recalled, the Stewarts' life had returned to normal.

She remembered the day they had emptied their savings account in order to make a down payment on a modest cottage at the edge of town, and how proud they had been that they had done this without help from his parents. Then the time had come to add to their family, and she had insisted that they first find a house with room for children, with a back yard and trees, and with all the things children need. He had agreed. Then, with joy and excitement, they had moved into the big old house on Maple Avenue, the one with the lilac bushes on either side of the driveway and the enormous veranda on the front. It had required work, of course, and paint and wallpaper were the least of it. But at last it had been done. When the nursery had been painted a sunny yellow and she had finished the last stitch on the curtains with the little orange ducks on them, she had said, "It's time. Everything is just perfect."

And so they had waited. And waited. Every month she prayed fervently : Please, God, let it be now. And every month she had bravely said, "Next time, maybe next time." Finally they had realized it was futile. They went to the doctor, who gave them the sad news that Betty could have no more children. The complications stemming from that difficult childbirth several years before had robbed her of what she had always thought was every woman's right.

Soon after that she slipped into despair. All night long she prowled the house, sighing and weeping. Even when she was taking care of Paul, she felt sad and empty. Paul would never have a brother or sister. Her life, once so full of hope, seemed a burden to her, and she often spoke of ending it.

Nothing in David's medical textbooks had prepared him for such a situation. All his years of study meant nothing to him now—everything he did seemed futile.

Then one day, an angel had appeared, a little angel. Very little, in fact. And he came to live with them and changed their lives.

Betty sat downstairs at the dining room table, a contented smile playing across her face. In front of her were stacks of freshly laundered little shirts, little pants, tiny little booties, and those stretchy little sleepers she could never fold quite right. In her lap lay a pile of soft white diapers, and she methodically picked them up one by one and creased them carefully, first once, then once again. Paul was in nursery school now, and she was often alone with Danny.

She turned toward the kitchen to check the clock over the refrigerator. It was almost time. He'd be waking up from his nap any minute now. She had never before stopped to think about how much little babies slept during the daytime, or, she chuckled, how little they slept at night. It seemed that Paul hadn't been that way. But no matter when babies woke up, they were always hungry. The bottles were all prepared and waiting in the fridge, and on her way she stopped to turn the burner on under the double boiler that she used for heating up formula.

Really, there's nothing to it, she congratulated herself. She was a mother for the second time and she was doing fine. She was able to balance the needs of both her children. With a practiced gesture, she squirted the bottle onto her wrist. Satisfied, she headed up the stairs and tiptoed toward the nursery.

She peered into the room and gazed lovingly at his bassinet under the window. A gentle breeze fluttered the curtains, and she almost laughed aloud as the ducks seemed to waddle up and down the fabric. From under his bunting she could glimpse a few wisps of coal black hair. How could anyone, she wondered, ever give up such a perfect little boy? I will never let him go, she promised with all her heart.

Silently she stole up to the bassinet. "Danny," she cooed softly, "Mommy's here."

He made no sound, so she reached down and

gently pulled back his bunting. "Oh, my God!" she screamed, paralyzed with fear. "What's happened?"

Penny Hughes was sweltering in the summer heat. Overhead, a fan lazily exchanged the warm air near the seats for the even hotter air at the ceiling. To make matters worse, the courtroom was packed. This was the trial of the season, and no one wanted to miss any of the sensational disclosures. The room rippled with the whirr of paper fans, and everyone had to strain to make out the testimony. What was absurd was that their rapt attention was so unnecessary. Anything they didn't hear was sure to be repeated a few hours later at dinner tables all over Oakdale. Furthermore, they could read all about it in any newspaper they picked up—not only *The Oakdale Gazette* but papers from all over the state had sent stringers to cover the goings-on.

Yesterday, the district attorney had scored major points in his battle to convict Jeff of Al James's murder. He called witness after witness, and one by one they told the same story—that Jeff Baker had quarrelled with the deceased, that Jeff Baker had threatened bodily harm to the deceased, and that Jeff Baker had gone off into the night in a blind rage. Later, they had heard a struggle and had rushed outside to the parking lot, where they saw Al James's body lying on the ground in a pool of blood and a dark figure hurtling off into the shadows.

The district attorney concluded his presentation of the state's case with a few eloquent remarks about the value of human life and the obligation of the jurors to inflict punishment on those who seized that precious gift of life from others. He then listed Jeff's previous problems with the police and reminded the jury of their duty to protect society from chronic lawbreakers. The day ended with the twelve grim-faced jurors resolutely filing out, leaving behind them a crowd of spectators sure that there was nothing Chris Hughes, the attorney, could do to prevent them from convicting Jeff of murder in the first degree.

Penny knew that her father specialized in corporate law and that he had limited experience in courtroom trials. In addition, this was his first murder case ever. Nonetheless she believed in him. Somehow he would find a way to save Jeff. He just had to.

Right now he was just finishing up his opening remarks, and the jury was listening with some skepticism as he reminded them that in the great United States of America, a man is considered innocent until proven guilty, and the case against Jeff Baker at this point was far from proven. Then, before he called his first witness, he made a request.

"Your honor, I respectfully ask for a brief recess so that I can confer with my client."

"It is unusual," the judge intoned, "so early in the day, but the request is granted."

Chris leaned over and whispered briefly in Jeff's ear. Jeff shook his head vehemently, adamant in his denial. Chris leaned in again and spoke firmly but so quietly that no one near them could overhear what they were discussing.

At one point, Chris glared fiercely into Jeff's eyes and slapped his hand on the table for emphasis. Jeff turned white, then he bowed his head and his shoulders began to shake. Chris patted him on the back and said, "Thank you, Jeff. You won't regret this. You're a good man."

Then he stood up and approached the bench. "Your honor," he said solemnly, "the defense would like to call its first witness. Miss Penny Hughes, will you please take the stand?"

Horror-stricken, Penny gripped the edge of her seat. "Why didn't you tell me?" she accused Nancy. "I'm not testifying. Anything I say is only going to make it worse. If he makes me get on the witness stand, I'll send Jeff to prison for life, or worse!"

"Miss Penny Hughes to the stand please," the clerk repeated.

Nancy took Penny's hand and held it tight. "Just trust in you father, dear, and everything will be all right. He knows what he's doing, even if you and I don't."

Reluctantly Penny walked forward and sat in the chair reserved for witnesses. As she put her hand on the Bible and almost inaudibly pledged to tell the truth, she scanned the jury box, hoping to find an open and compassionate face. Dejected, she shifted her gaze to her father, who now stood before her.

Gently he reminded her of her oath and suggested that she listen carefully to each question and consider thoroughly each answer before she gave it. Then he led her through an account of the events of that awful evening so many months ago, sparing no details. Her heart ached as she heard herself corroborate each and every statement of the prosecution's witnesses. Then she was forced to tell the court about the most personally painful part of the night, when she made Jeff take her home, and she watched him drive off alone. Finally it was over, and Penny drew a deep breath.

Why had he done this? Penny's mind was a muddle of conflicting emotions. She could barely stand to believe it, but perhaps he saw his chance to rid the Hughes family of Jeff forever. Why had she trusted him? It was more than she could bear to accept right now, that she had been betrayed by her own father. And sooner or later she would have to find the strength to confront him about it. But at this very moment all she could think about doing was escaping the prying eyes of the judge and jury.

"Just a moment, your honor." That was the district attorney. His uncompromising tone stopped Penny from leaving the stand. "I believe I have the right to cross-examine this witness."

Her heart sank. Her testimony under her father's guidance had been damaging enough, but this could quite literally be the kiss of death for Jeff. It was astonishing to her that the paths of so many lives could be changed so quickly, and so needlessly. If only she'd stayed by Jeff's side that night! Then none of this ever would have happened.

It was in that moment that she knew her future was with Jeff, no matter what the outcome of the trial. Whether he was found innocent or guilty, she would stick by him. He deserved at least that much from her, especially after what she had done. He would have been much better off if she had just disappeared before the trial had begun. That way, she, his most friendly witness, would not have had to confirm the mounting evidence against him, and she would not have been compelled to add detail after damning detail. But there was no turning back now. Her treatment at the hands of her own father, inexplicable as it was, had been bad enough—what she now faced could only be worse.

The time had finally come for Penny to acknowledge publicly what she had kept hidden from herself these many months—that she believed Jeff was guilty. She drove a knife through her heart as she admitted this to herself, but it was true. All the evidence pointed to it, and the most damaging testimony had come from her own lips. There was no avoiding it. She, Penny Hughes, was in love with a murderer. And not only had she failed to prevent him from committing his crime, now she was ensuring that he paid for it with his life.

She waited. The district attorney paced back and forth. When at last he spoke, Penny jumped. "Your honor," he said, "I have no questions."

David Stewart yanked open the door and bounded up the stairs. Moments after he had received his wife's frantic phone call, he left the lab at the hospital and sped for home. He turned the corner in his hallway and dashed into the nursery, where Betty stood, mute and stricken, over the bassinet. Automatically he flung off his jacket, loosened his tie, and rolled up his sleeves. Brusquely shoving her aside, he reached down to pick up the motionless infant.

Without warning he began to chuckle, then he laughed heartily. The baby, awakened so suddenly, gave forth with a lusty cry. Betty stared, transfixed and uncomprehending. David unzipped the bunting and slipped the tiny body into his arms.

"Spots!" Betty cried. "He's all covered with spots! What's wrong with him?"

"Betty, sweetheart," David said, relieved, "please relax. It's nothing serious. It's only a little heat rash, and all babies get it. You see, it's very hot today, and you've got him all bundled up here, and his little pores can't breathe. That's the only thing that's wrong."

"Well, what should we do? Should I call the doctor?" Betty was already on her way to the phone.

"I am a doctor, remember?" He couldn't wipe the grin off his face no matter how hard he tried. "And I know just what to do. So don't worry. We'll give this little fella a nice cool bath, and we'll put some baking soda in the water, and all these nasty spots will go right away."

"They taught you about baking soda in medical school?" Betty was still not convinced.

"No, I learned it from the best pediatrician I ever knew—my own mother."

After the bath, they took the baby downstairs, and Betty held him and gave him a bottle. Defeat was etched across her brow. "Maybe I'm just not cut out for motherhood," she confessed. "Is there something wrong with me? Aren't women supposed to have an instinct for all this?"

David put his arm around her. "Let me tell you

a little secret. Nobody, and I mean nobody, has an easy time of it. Parenthood requires an enormous adjustment, and lots of things come up that nobody knows how to handle. It just takes experience. That's why God, in his infinite wisdom, saves the really tough problems for later. If you think today was difficult, just you wait till our little Dan is a teenager."

"My heart says you're right, but my mind keeps saying something else. Oh, David, if only . . ." She paused, then sighed from the very depths of her soul. "If only I was his real mother."

"You stop that kind of talk this instant!" he ordered sharply. "You are his real mother for all intents and purposes. When his biological mother gave him up, she also gave up all claim to him, and you became his mother. You're the only mother he'll ever know, and I'm his only dad. We're good parents, too, and we'll get even better."

Betty looked down at the tiny bundle of energy squirming in her arms, and her eyes misted over with tears. "How could anyone part with such a wonderful baby?" she murmured, part in anger, part in gratitude. "What kind of woman would do such a thing?"

"Can I see him now?" There was an air of unreality to Ellen's question to the nurse at Oakdale Memorial Hospital. Tim Cole had finally become Ellen's husband, but now she had to ask for permission to see him. First there had been the separation from their baby when Ellen had given him up for adoption, and now there was this separation . . .

It was some cruel twist of fate that gave a total stranger power over whether or not a wife could see a husband, she felt, and each time there was an unfamiliar nurse at the station, Ellen's heart jumped to her throat before she could introduce herself. "I'm Mrs. Tim Cole," she would say, choking down the fear, her new name strange on her tongue. "He's in Room 512. May I see him, please?" And each day, the nurse on duty would say, "Yes, Mrs. Cole. You may go right in."

And so Ellen waited for the usual okay while the lady behind the desk checked her clipboard. But today the nurse looked up and curtly announced, "Dr. Cole has been transferred. He's no longer in 512."

"Where is he, please?" Ellen inquired.

"I don't know, ma'am. He's no longer on this floor."

Ellen trembled slightly with the barest beginnings of panic. "What floor is he on, please?"

"Just a moment." The nurse picked up the telephone, dialed, spoke briefly, and hung up. Then she buried herself in her paperwork and didn't even raise her head when she said, "I.C.U."

Ellen was at the elevator in a flash. I.C.U.— that was two floors down, she remembered, as she frantically jabbed at the call button. When the doors began to slide open, she pushed them aside, as if that gesture would make them move faster.

"Doctor!" she called, spotting him before the doors were fully open. "My husband. What's wrong?"

"Mrs. Cole, I just had you paged. Could you step in here please?" he requested, motioning toward the swinging double doors.

Ellen stumbled blindly forward, the enormity of her husband's illness hitting her suddenly. She glanced around the room, vainly searching for a recognizable form. At last she saw Tim, over in the corner, barely visible under the tubes and wires, and she knew in her heart what lay ahead. But she could not accept it fully. All she knew was their happy marriage, so brief and so fraught with pain, did not deserve to end like this, in some anonymous room with gray walls and machinery. In agony and rage Ellen cried out, "No!" but not a sound came forth.

From nowhere her mother appeared and put her arm around her. Ellen's head fell to Claire's shoulder—her light brown hair cascaded down over her mother's bosom. Together they stood, hushed and solemn. The inevitability of death carries on awesome weight, and they both felt its crushing burden.

"I'm sorry," Claire said simply. "I came as soon as I heard."

"It's so unfair! We had so little time together."

A doctor scurried past them, a nurse at his heels. Together they bent over Tim, and the nurse scribbled on her chart as the doctor hurriedly barked out orders. Then they exited as quickly as they'd entered, and Ellen and Claire were left alone at his bedside.

"They're doing everything they can," Claire offered, aware that there was really nothing she could say.

"We had so little time together," Ellen

repeated, almost to herself. "So little time."

"That's right, dear, but those days were filled with happiness. Try to remember him as he was then, instead of like this." Alien sights and sounds filled the room, and Claire knew that her daughter must feel much more disoriented than she did. Ellen's only hope of getting through this was to concentrate on what went well in her relationship with Tim, and Claire realized she must help her focus on the good moments they had so recently shared.

"I know, Mom. The day he told me we could be together, to be man and wife at last, I was so filled with joy I thought I'd burst. And he was so handsome and proud. All our troubles were over, he said, because his wife had finally agreed to give him a divorce. Oh, the plans we made! The wedding, where we'd live, it was all so wonderful!" Ellen seemed to be gaining strength with each word.

"We had our wedding, too, didn't we? And we vowed that from that day forward, we would only look to the future, never to the past," she continued, slowly becoming aware that a large part of her life was being snatched from her. "Oh, where will I find the courage to keep that promise now? When Tim is gone, what will I have left?"

"You'll have yourself, dear, with all your wonderful qualities of compassion and faith and, yes, courage. I know that your life hasn't been easy, and I know, too, that your father and I have contributed greatly to the pain you've suffered over the years. But I'm a survivor, Ellen, and you're my daughter, and you're a survivor too. It may not seem like it now, but you'll get through this. It will end, I guarantee you, and you will go on. Someday you'll even be able to have a good, fruitful life." Claire was speaking as much to herself as to her daughter, she knew. If only she and Jim had been honest from the beginning, if only they had not allowed his affair with Edith to poison their home, then . . . But it was too late for all of that now. Claire was picking up the pieces of her life, and soon Ellen would be able to do the same. Still, with a mother's heavy heart, she regretted how she'd handled her life in the past, and she cursed herself for her weakness.

Two doctors came in, paced by a nurse reading from her chart. One of the doctors took Ellen aside and said, "We have some test results and we're just waiting for some more. One of the doctors had to leave on an emergency, but I'm sure it will be only another minute or two. We've known for some time that your husband's blood disease was extremely rare, and what we're looking for here is some way we might possibly treat it. We're not giving up, Mrs. Cole, and you shouldn't either."

This was the first time in days that anyone had offered Ellen even the tiniest ray of hope, and she seized it. Perhaps Tim would live. "Oh, Mom, did you hear that?" She whirled around, elated, to hug her mother. "He said there was still some chance that . . ."

"Now, if you ladies will excuse us," he interrupted gently, "we have work to do."

The waiting room glowed with a warmth and cheer Ellen hadn't noticed before, and as she sat next to her mother, she felt infused with optimism and trust. The minutes stretched to hours, yet she gaily chattered on, first regaling her mother with stories of things she and Tim had done in the past, then entertaining her with plans for things they'd promised to do in the future. Before they knew it, it was late afternoon, and the growling in their stomachs reminded them they hadn't eaten since breakfast.

"We'll be in the cafeteria if there's any news," Ellen informed the nurse at the desk, "and then we're coming right back."

"Just a moment, please, Mrs. Cole." It was the doctor, who'd suddenly appeared behind her. His shoulders sagged and his face was ashen.

"What is it? Is it Tim? Is he still . . ?"

The doctor shook his head and muttered bleakly, "We tried everything we knew but we couldn't save him. I'm truly very sorry."

Ellen felt her knees buckle, and she dimly perceived two strong arms catching her and breaking her fall. When she woke up, she was on a gurney being wheeled down the hall. Doctors and nurses surrounded her, and she could barely make out her mother's face in the crowd.

"Are you all right, Mrs. Cole?" someone asked.

"Can you hear me?" another queried.

"Ellen, don't worry. You just fainted, and you're going to be just fine." Her mother's voice cut through the confusion and restored Ellen to reality.

"Stop!" she commanded, sitting up straight. "Stop! You're not taking me anywhere!" Before anyone could prevent her, she hopped off the gurney and was running down the corridor as fast as her legs would carry her.

Tim was dead, and nothing could change that

horrible reality. Her mother was right—she had to look ahead. But before she could do that, she must go back to the past. She couldn't face the future until she'd first stopped to retrieve something precious she had left behind.

Penny had rushed out of the courtroom, certain she had sealed Jeff's fate. Through the doors, down the hall and the stairs, and out the front she fled, until at last she was free.

Then it hit. The afternoon heat came at her like a wall of fire. The sidewalk shimmered, and the pavement seemed to move beneath her feet. Yet still she walked, for hours and hours, unable to shake the ugly knowledge that she'd destroyed the man she loved, first by allowing him to commit a crime for which he must pay, and then by revealing in court the very evidence that would convict him. Penny could not conceive of a life without Jeff. She hadn't told her parents yet, but they'd planned to be married again, to raise a family together, and to spend the rest of their lives as one happy unit. Now all their dreams were shattered, and Penny had no urge to pick up the pieces of her life and move on.

She walked and walked, until finally the waning sun brought temporary relief from the oppressive heat. She trudged back toward the courthouse to meet her mother, in spite of the fact that she wasn't at all anxious to see her father. What he'd done still rankled, though Penny understood the fault wasn't his. As an officer of the court, he did have an obligation to bring out the truth, though for the life of her, she couldn't understand how he could abandon

Jeff's interests so completely. One day she would find the words to tell her father how she felt, but for now all she wanted was to go home and rest.

"Penny! Penny, where have you been?" Her mother was standing across the street on the steps of the courthouse, frantically waving at her and motioning her to hurry. Then she yelled something, but it was unintelligible over the din of the rush hour traffic.

Penny crossed the street. "What?" she asked weakly.

"I've been looking for you for hours. You just disappeared, and I didn't know where to find you." Nancy's cheeks were flushed, and she spoke swiftly as she took Penny's elbow and hustled her up the steps. "Your father completed his case soon after you left, and now the jury has reached a decision. We never expected it this fast—they've only been in deliberation for an hour or so. Maybe it's a good sign."

Or a terrible omen, thought Penny dismally. The district attorney's case was so airtight that there was simply no room for doubt. But she was powerless to prevent herself from being carried along by Nancy's enthusiasm, and moments later they entered the courtroom at full speed.

Nancy sat directly behind Chris, gripping his shoulder as the tension built. Penny sat in the back of the room, averting her eyes as the jurors quickly marched into their seats. She didn't dare search their faces for a clue to their decision.

The foreman stood. The moment of truth was at hand. Penny contemplated putting her hands over her ears, then at the very last second, thought better of it. She might as well face the truth.

"We have reached a verdict, your honor," he was saying. "We, the jury, find the defendant, Jeff Baker . . ."

The rest of his words were drowned out in shouting. The judge vainly pounded his gavel for order, and eventually the spectators fell silent. Penny sat forward, straining to hear.

"We, the jury," he repeated, "find the defendant, Jeff Baker, not guilty" and the courtroom erupted in pandemonium. Penny couldn't believe her ears. How had this happened? Slowly she made her way forward through the cheering throng. Jeff had his arms around Chris, giving him a big bear hug. Nancy stood next to them, beaming with pride. When Jeff spotted Penny, he broke free from Chris and rushed to her.

"Thank you, my darling!" he crowed exultantly. "I owe it all to you."

"What are you talking about? I don't understand." Her head was spinning.

"It was your testimony that got me off, you little dummy. Because of what you said, the jury realized I couldn't have murdered Al James." He picked her up and twirled her around, laughing joyously.

Nancy saw the confusion on her daughter's face. "You told the jury that Jeff had left you off at our house, and you told them what time. You rushed out of the courtroom after you were done, or else you'd know what happened next. Something clicked inside your father's head, and he began recalling all those prosecution witnesses. That's when he discovered that Al

James was killed at exactly the time Jeff dropped you off. Therefore Jeff couldn't have done it." Nancy glanced at Chris with love. "It was really so simple. That is, if you've got a brilliant legal mind."

Penny put her arms around Jeff's neck. "Jeff, now we can have the life we've always dreamed of. I've got—I mean, we've got the greatest parents in the whole wide world."

Chapter Six
A Wedding

It was unusual not to have snow in Oakdale by Christmastime, but after the miserable weather of last year, no one was complaining. No one, that is, except Penny. If it would just hurry up and snow already, she thought, then Jeff would stop singing "White Christmas."

Penny slid lower into the seat of Jeff's car. "It's not too late to call off the wedding, you know," she teased. "Do you sing in the shower?"

"I sing when I'm happy," he chortled.

"Then we're in deep trouble, because something tells me you're going to be ecstatically happy for a long, long time."

"You mean because your parents are helping us get a car?" he inquired innocently, reaching over to draw her closer to him.

"Get your hand back on the wheel and drive. You know perfectly well what I'm referring to, Mr. Jeff Baker. I'm referring to our upcoming nuptials which, in case you've forgotten, are tomorrow."

"My gosh, really? Well, we'd better get cracking then, hadn't we?"

Penny excitedly pointed off to the side. "Oh, Jeff, look. All those Christmas trees. Can't we buy one please? I don't want to wait a whole year before we have our very own tree. Please let's stop and get one now."

"Sure," he agreed, "but where would we put it? Right next to your parents' tree? I don't think there's room."

"It was just a thought." She stuck out her lower lip in an exaggerated pout. Shopping for cars was much more fun for Jeff than it was for her, and she was beginning to feel bored. They'd been at it since after lunch, and by now she was feeling chilled to the bone and hungry, to boot. They'd have to call it quits in a few minutes anyway, and she wished he'd just head for home right now. But it was so important to him, she knew, and it had been awfully nice of her folks to give them a down payment as a wedding present.

Jeff braked hard and swung into a brightly lit used car lot. "That's it! Over there, do you see it? The red one, against the fence."

"Jeff, its a convertible." Her tone was as withering as she could make it, which was not very. "Not very practical for these Illinois winters."

"But look at it, honey. It's the best-looking car we've seen." He had parked and was already halfway out the door.

Reluctantly she followed him. "Why don't we look at something a little less racy? Something with four doors, maybe even a station wagon."

"A station wagon!" he hooted. "What on earth would we do with a station wagon?"

"Jeff, we've already discussed this," she pleaded. It embarrassed her to discuss something so personal in public, but she plunged ahead anyway. "We agreed we'd start a family right away, and that's why my parents gave us money to use towards a car. You don't want your son to be riding around Oakdale in your old jalopy, do you?" She snuggled up to him to ward off the cold.

"I know, but just let me look." Cars were Jeff's passion, and he could never resist checking them out. He strode over to the convertible and inspected it with a practiced eye. First he ran his fingers over the finish, then got down on his knees and examined the side. Then he reached over and grabbed the front tire and tried to shake it. It didn't budge. He walked to the rear and performed the same operation. Finally he was satisfied and stood up and brushed off his hands. "She's clean, never been in a wreck," he announced. "Let's take her for a spin."

Penny was weakening by the moment as his enthusiasm built. "Oh, all right," she said as she smiled indulgently. Perhaps the station wagon could come later, she supposed. Just because you're married doesn't mean you're dead.

For the first time in many years, Nancy Hughes felt out of control. Her eldest daughter was getting married in less than twenty-four hours, and there was still so much to be done. She'd thought she had all the details taken care of, but now everything seemed to be going awry. The rehearsal was in a couple of hours, and they had to eat dinner first and then get to the church to run through the ceremony. And no one was even home yet. Penny and her intended had been out all day; Chris wasn't home from the office, and Donald had appeared and then disappeared. Grandpa was off somewhere on some mysterious errand he refused to discuss. Only the youngest two were showing any evidence of that famous Hughes reliability. After setting the table, they'd both gone upstairs, Bobby to play and Susan to read.

Nancy took out a pencil and paper and sat down to make a list of the things she wanted to check on. When she and Chris had agreed to give Penny a big church wedding, she'd thought only of how beautiful it would be, not of how much work it would entail. She and Penny had been toiling away for weeks, and the end was in sight only because there was nearly no time left, not because everything had been completed to her satisfaction. There were the flower arrangements, which had to be done at the last minute, the food for the reception, which also couldn't be completed too far in advance, and so many minor details it boggled her mind. Thank heavens she'd finished all the fittings. The last thing she wanted to do was to take up needle and thread. She rested her chin on her hand and surveyed the kitchen. In all her years of married life, she'd never seen the kitchen in such disarray, and she was too exhausted to care.

All at once her peace and quiet was shattered as a raucous commotion broke out in the driveway. She jumped up and dashed out the door to see what was the matter. Chris, Grandpa, Donald, and Ellen were all clustered around a red convertible Nancy had never seen before. Penny was sitting in the passenger seat trying to look displeased but not succeeding, while Jeff was standing with one foot on the driver's seat and the other on the steering wheel. He appeared to be quoting something, but Nancy couldn't make out what it was. Judging from the appreciative reaction of his audience, she realized it had to be some sort of poem he was mangling for the occasion.

"Enough!" laughed Chris. "Let's eat." He turned and headed for the porch, spied Nancy, and gave her a big smooch on the cheek before going in the door.

"That's right, dinner's ready. Everyone, come on in," she called. "Penny, your cheeks are all red. You look frozen. Jeff, you get your fiancée inside this instant." Grandpa scurried past her without a word, Jeff and Penny at his heels. "Hurry, hurry, I'm getting goose bumps," she complained.

Ellen slipped her arm through Donald's and whispered something in his ear.

"I know. Do you think we'll ever be so ridiculously happy?" he asked as they dawdled though the door.

Nancy headed for the stove. "Everyone in the dining room in ten minutes, and no exceptions. We've got quite a schedule to keep if we want to have everything ready for the big day tomorrow."

Penny woke up with butterflies in her stomach, the biggest butterflies she'd ever felt. This was the last morning in her life that she would ever be Penny Hughes. From now on she would be Penny Baker or, more properly, Mrs. Jeff Baker. She liked the ring of it, and it was becoming much more familiar to her. It should be, for she'd repeated her new name to herself thousands of times over the past few months. At first it had sounded merely wonderful, and then as time wore on, it had come to portend a whole magical new life. They'd weathered storm after storm and had emerged as full-grown, confident adults committed to spending the rest of their lives in each other's arms. All in all, it was a very nice feeling, Penny thought as she slipped on her robe.

At the bottom of the stairs she stopped and pulled back the curtain on the little window next to the front door. It was snowing! Crisp, light flurries floated down from the sky and dusted the earth, leaving it with a fresh, pure look that struck Penny as being just exactly right for the day's events. She hurried to the telephone and dialed Jeff.

"I know I probably shouldn't be talking to you this morning because it's bad luck or something, but you've just got to look out the window," she babbled the moment he had picked up the receiver.

"Hunh?" he yawned.

"Your dream came true, Jeff. Remember what you were singing yesterday?"

"Hunh?"

"White Christmas. You were singing I'm Dreaming of a White Christmas. Well, drag yourself up to the window and look outside."

Jeff whooped in joy. "Baby, our lives are just starting! I love you. Can I come over?"

"No, you can't, and I shouldn't even be talking to you. Goodbye," she giggled as she hung up the phone. Filled with excitement and anticipation, she danced into the kitchen to start the percolator. She whirled through the dining room, leaped over the threshold, took one final spin, and landed directly in her mother's open arms.

"Mom! What are you doing up so early?" she gasped in surprise.

"Not much, dear. Just thought I'd get up and see if anything special was going on today," Nancy replied dryly, as she reached in the cabinet for another coffee cup. "Here, dear, sit down and drink this. I want to have a little chat with you."

"Oh, goody. I was afraid that in all the frenzy around here you'd have forgotten. We're definitely due for that traditional mother-daughter talk." Penny winked slyly. "You first."

"Try to be serious about this. This is a big step you're taking. Marriage is very different from just dating someone. It's a major responsibility that lasts a lifetime, and frankly, it doesn't really get easier. After you have children of your own, you'll understand what I mean. You and Jeff are making a commitment not only to share your lives together, but also to stand by each other when things aren't so pleasant. No marriage is perfect, you know. I suppose your father and I have about as good a marriage as two people could ever hope to have, but we certainly have had our disagreements, and some of them have been pretty bad. When you children were younger, we pretty much agreed on how you should be raised. But as you got older, the questions you brought to us were nowhere near as simple, and quite often Chris and I came up with very different answers. What we had to learn to do was to compromise, dear, and I guess that's what I'm trying to tell you about now. You and Jeff should discuss things and listen to each other, but just because you're man and wife doesn't mean you should stop looking into your own heart. Love him and respect him, Penny, but do the same for yourself. Compromise doesn't mean blindly following another person's lead—it means finding a common ground between what two separate people believe. Have faith in yourself, dear, and you'll lead a happy and productive life." She reached over and grasped Penny's hands. "I love you."

"Is that it?" Penny grimaced in mock disappointment. "I thought you were going to tell me about . . . you know, about . . . men."

"Men?" Chris strode in. "Here's a man. Here are two, in fact," he declared as Don appeared.

Penny turned a deep crimson. "Good morning, Daddy. Mother and I were just talking."

"Did I interrupt something? Don't worry, Don and I will be out of here in a minute, won't we, Don? Donald?"

"Oh, sorry, Dad. What did you say? I was just thinking about something."

Nancy stood up and crossed to the stove. "Never mind, Chris. Let's all have some breakfast. Penny and I were all done, really we were."

It seemed as if all of Oakdale were there, decked out in their winter finery to witness the union of Penny Hughes and Jeff Baker. Yet for such a large wedding, it had a remarkably intimate and personal feel. The area around the altar was transformed into a bower replete with fragrant buds of every type of flower Nancy could find. The wedding party was small, just the two families, and Susan in particular was thrilled to have been asked to be the flower girl.

Penny was radiant, her hair pulled back from her glowing face and her veil simple and stylishly restrained. Deep in the scalloped v-neck of her flowing white gown gleamed a gold necklace with one perfect pearl hanging from it. This was her gift from Jeff, and she knew she would treasure it always.

Jeff stood tall and uncharacteristically reverent. In honor of the occasion he'd consented to wear a white carnation in his lapel, and he hadn't even put up much of a fuss. For the moment he was quite subdued, with just a hint of his trademark mischief lurking beneath the surface. He and Penny listened intently as the minister read the service. At the appointed moment he slipped the ring on her finger and they recited their vows, gazing deeply into each other's eyes.

Nancy took out her handkerchief and dabbed at the two tiny tears that were threatening to roll down her cheeks. Crying at weddings, she thought, is so typical, especially for the mother of the bride. She sniffed loudly and returned her attention to the altar.

"You may now kiss the bride," the minister was saying.

Jeff bent forward slightly, took Penny in his arms, and kissed her lightly and sweetly on the lips. An appreciative murmur swept through the crowd. Then without warning he grasped Penny sturdily and dipped her low, planting a firm kiss on her open mouth. Penny flushed as she came up for air, and everyone began to laugh. The solemnity was broken, and she was now and forever the proud Mr. Jeff Baker.

By the time everyone arrived at the reception, Jeff was in fine form. No one was surprised when he took the obligatory first slice of cake and smeared it across her chin, but it was Penny's reaction that brought the hilarity to its highest pitch. With her finger she took a daub of icing, aimed it sweetly at his lips, then carefully and deliberately wiped it up the bridge of his nose. Before he had a chance to retaliate, she stood on her tiptoes and kissed him, saying, "You're incorrigible, Jeff, do you know that? And from now on, I am too. Now let's serve this cake so we can get to the presents."

Nancy slipped off her shoes and plopped them squarely on the coffee table. "I'm worn to a frazzle," she announced to no one in particular. "The next time there's a wedding in this family, I'm personally seeing to it that it doesn't coincide with a holiday."

"Aw, Mom, I had my heart set on getting married on Arbor Day," Donald teased.

Nancy sat up. "Dear," she inquired sharply, "does that mean that you and Ellen are becoming serious?"

"Yes, Mom, you know we are. But don't worry, it's still a little premature to discuss an actual date. I was only kidding."

"Pardon me, but I wonder if I could have the floor for a moment." Grandpa stood up with a flourish. "We're not quite done with this wedding, so let's put off planning the next one until we are. Penny and Jeff, front and center, please. Your grandfather has a gift for you." He reached into the inside pocket of his coat and drew out an envelope.

"Oh, Grandpa, a check! How sweet of you!" Penny opened her palm.

"My, you're quick, Mrs. Baker," he said as he placed the envelope squarely in Jeff's hand.

"Jeff, let me open it," she squealed. "All I got to unwrap today were three toasters." Shriveling under his glance, she added lamely, "And a few other things, too numerous to mention."

"Honey, look!" he exclaimed. "It's . . . it's . . . What is it?"

Grandpa chuckled delightedly, enjoying the suspense his gift was creating. "It's a reservation voucher, Jeff. You and your bride will enjoy a romantic vacation, starting the day after tomorrow, right after Christmas, in the honeymoon suite at one of the finest hotels in Miami Beach, Florida. And this," he continued, holding aloft another envelope, "contains airline tickets to get you there."

"Grandpa, I don't know what to say," Penny stammered.

"Please don't say anything yet," he replied. "I'm not done." He paused to take a long, drawn-out breath. "This final envelope, and it really is the last one, I promise you," he said as he produced yet another one, "holds a small check to ensure that you don't starve to death on that warm and sunny beach."

Penny threw her arms around his neck. "Grandpa, you're too much, and I love you and thank you. And Jeff thanks you too, right, sweetheart?"

Jeff blushed. "Yup," he grinned. "I will. I mean, I do."

Two days later, the Hughes house was quieter than it had been for months. Chris was at the office, and Donald had taken the newlyweds to the airport. Nancy sat in the kitchen, sampling this rare breather from her hectic schedule. Her first child, her little Penny, had left the nest. My, how time flies, she thought. And soon, it will be Donald, then probably Bobby, then Susan. This is what motherhood is all about, she told herself. You raise your children, you do your very best to teach them the difference between right and wrong, and you let them go. And then you sit home alone and it hurts. She gazed at the now sparkling countertops, and longed for the disorganized clutter of the past few weeks. A part of Penny's life was just beginning, but a part of her own was ending, and it brought emotions she hadn't yet adjusted to.

Feeling sorry for herself was not one of Nancy's favorite pastimes, so it was with relief that she heard Donald pull into the driveway. She stood up quickly and busied herself at the sink.

"Hello, dear," she called over her shoulder as

he entered. "Did they get off okay?"

"Everything went like a charm, Mom. Did Ellen call?"

"No, she didn't. Were you expecting her to?"

"Well, kind of. I was hoping we'd make some plans for New Year's Eve." Donald opened the refrigerator and took out a plate of leftover chicken.

"Let me do that for you, dear, while you tell me all about you and Ellen. With all the excitement around here, I feel I've neglected you. How are things going?"

"Much better, really, Mom," Donald allowed. "At first it was rough, what with all that Ellen's been through lately. Her parents' problems affected her a great deal, and you know, I think the way her father had behaved towards her mother had made her distrust men somewhat. But I feel we've worked through that. And then of course Tim's death was quite a blow. She'll never forget him, but I don't think his memory will stand in the way of our relationship any longer. She felt so guilty over the way things turned out for them, even though it wasn't her fault at all. I guess it was very difficult for her to get past those feelings—and for me to help her do that. But now I really think I see the light at the end of the tunnel, and I think Ellen does too. She's finally ready to start living again—she's making a new beginning, and I'm going to be part of that. This coming year will be the year for Ellen and me—I can feel it."

Nancy handed him a plate of sliced chicken, then set down silverware and a paper napkin. "I'm so glad you've found someone you care about. The wedding made me realize how precious love is and how, when two people really love each other, they should be together no matter what. So I hope everything works out for you and Ellen, dear. I really do."

"It will. As a matter of fact, I'm going to call her right now. Maybe I can persuade her to go out to dinner with me." He bounced jauntily to the telephone.

"Hello, Mrs. Lowell, how are you?" he inquired. "Did you have a nice holiday?" He listened politely for several minutes, then asked, "Could I speak to Ellen, please?"

"Donald," came her mystified reply, "didn't Ellen tell you? She left for Europe this morning. She won't be back for months."

Penny gaped out the open window. She'd never seen anything like it. Why had no one ever told her how truly beautiful Florida was? The sand formed a glowing white ribbon next to the mysterious dark form of the ocean. Moonlight glinted off the water, and in the shimmering shapes Penny could see exotic patterns emerging.

"Jeff, look! Turn off the light and come and see."

He stood directly behind her, his arms encircling her. She leaned back, and together they swayed in the balmy breeze. The intoxicating aroma of lush tropical vegetation wafted up to them, and they drank it in hungrily. After what seemed an eternity, Jeff slowly and gently led her away from the window. "Penny, I love you," he said, his voice low and urgent.

"Jeff," she breathed, as she melted into his

embrace. "Oh, Jeff."

The crashing surf pounded rhythmically on the shore, but the two lovers were oblivious to everything except their own private world. Together they lay, invulnerable, inaccessible. They existed only for each other, and they luxuriated in their selfishness. Oakdale and the real world were only distant memories.

Chapter Seven
A Shocking Discovery

It looks just the same, mused Ellen as she stepped down from the train, almost as if I had never left. So much has happened to me over the past year that I've become practically a new person, she chuckled. Yet here in Oakdale it's almost as if time has stood still. I hope you're ready for the new Ellen Lowell, she announced silently to the whole population of Oakdale.

The porter handed down her bags as she scanned the platform for a familiar face. Surely her mother had received her telegram and had sent someone to meet her if she couldn't come herself. Ellen had made her plans somewhat at the last minute, she admitted, but still it would be nice to get a ride home from someone she knew instead of from one of the infamous Oakdale taxicabs.

"All aboard!"

Ellen gathered her luggage and stood back. How many times she'd heard that loud call lately, and in how many different languages! Europe had been such an adventure, yet when all was said and done, that was the least of its appeal for Ellen. For all the miles she had traveled on land, sea, and air, she had journeyed a far greater distance within her own mind.

She tried to remember when it had been that she'd first felt the shift within herself, the moment she realized fully that she was not bound by all that had happened before. The past didn't have to control her present or her future. She could be a free agent, doing what she wanted now, not limited by what she'd done in years gone by.

Had it been in Amsterdam that she'd first noticed the beginnings of a new direction? There she had gazed deeply into the paintings of Vermeer and Van Gogh. From one she'd felt subtlety and maturity, and from the other, dynamism and bright prospects. Had it been in Germany, on that train, which, after climbing the cold and austere Bavarian Alps, suddenly emerged into the sunshine and warmth of the Italian countryside? Or was it in Rome that the sense of self-renewal had become so overpowering? There on the Via Veneto she'd sat, sipping espresso and watching the tourists, as the Eternal City metamorphosized around her. Smartly dressed women shared the sidewalk with monks costumed as they had been for centuries, and modern shops and gleaming office buildings rose next to age-old ruins. To Ellen one fact emerged clearly—the past was a building block, not a stumbling block. It was something to be used if needed, or discarded if no longer valuable. And Ellen knew with certainty, as she stood there on the train platform in Oakdale, that her mind was crowded with relics from days gone by. From her parents' unhappy marriage to her own ill-fated alliance with Tim, which ended too soon after finally blossoming into a healthy relationship, she had been controlled by experiences that no longer had the power to rule her. She had to rid herself of those obsolete problems and compulsions. That was why she had returned to Oakdale. She had to face her past and retrieve from it what she needed.

"Mrs. Cole? Ellen Cole, is that you?"

Ellen turned puzzled. Virtually no one in Oakdale knew her as Tim's wife—they had been married such a short time before his death that she hadn't even adjusted to the loss of her maiden name. Her passport had been drawn in the name of Lowell, and for all these past months throughout Europe, she had passed herself off as Miss Ellen Lowell. Now only moments after her arrival home, she realized her true status as a widow.

Standing in front of her was a man she couldn't recall ever having seen before. Tall and handsome, but with a kindly air, he seemed amused at her confusion. "We met at the hospital," he explained with a shy grin, "during your husband's illness. I'm Dr. David Stewart."

"I'm sorry, but I still don't . . ." Ellen began, as she pulled her cashmere coat just a bit tighter around her waist.

"Of course you don't remember me. How silly of me. I work in the lab and I analyzed some tests for your husband—um, rather, your late husband. I know it's a little late for condolences, but I'd like to offer mine. Medical science has made marvelous progress, but there are times when even the latest advances somehow are inadequate. I'm very sorry. I only wish that . . . that . . ." he stammered. "Why are we standing here in the cold like this? Can I offer you a ride somewhere?"

"I'm not sure. I mean I don't know. I mean maybe," Ellen blurted out, then broke off laughing. "We certainly are having our difficulties with the English language today, aren't we? The truth is, I'd expected my mother to meet me, but I'm afraid my cable may have arrived too late. Lately I've become a spur-of-the-moment traveler, and I didn't give her much notice. I'd love a ride, but could you just wait a minute while I try to give her a call?"

Ellen stepped to the side of the platform and paused in front of the booth to search her purse for coins. After several seconds, she found a handful of change, inspected it, then looked up in chagrin. "Three lira, ten guilder, and a London trolley token. I'm definitely quite the world adventurer, don't you think? What country did you say this was, señor?"

"It'll be Iceland if we stay here any longer. Surely if your mother had gotten your telegram, she'd have been here to meet you, or at least she'd have sent someone. Why don't I just give you a lift home?"

"That would be wonderful, but aren't you already here to meet someone? I don't want to throw off your plans."

David smiled. "I was just dropping off some

passengers. My wife and two little boys are on their way to visit my in-laws for a few days, and I'm not due back at the hospital for the rest of the day, so I have plenty of time to take you wherever you need to go."

Within moments, they'd loaded Ellen's luggage into the Stewarts' station wagon and were making their way to the Lowell home near the country club. "Do you plan to stay here in Oakdale, or is this just another stop for you?" David asked as he skillfully drove the car through the mid-day traffic.

"I'm back for good," Ellen declared decisively. "I've unfinished business here."

"I love it when you come home for lunch!" squealed Penny as she stood on her tiptoes to pinch Jeff on his cheek. Deftly she whipped off her apron and tossed it on the kitchen table before giving him an impulsive hug.

"What's gotten into you today?" Jeff laughed, then regretted the question the moment he'd asked it. Quickly covering his thoughtlessness, he said, "I came home to take you out. Where do you want to go?"

"Nonsense, honey. Everything's all ready. I've made vegetable soup and a salad and I'm going to grill some tomato-and-cheese sandwiches just as soon as I've had a chance to greet my husband properly." With that she pulled Jeff to her and gave him a long, fervent kiss.

"You know what that does to me," he growled roguishly, "but I only have time for lunch."

"I know." The playfulness faded from her voice. "I missed you today and I'm glad you're here with me. Some days, Jeff, I just . . ." she murmured, barely audible, as she stared deep into his eyes. Softly, carefully, he folded his arms around her and held her. In silence they stood, motionless, linked by the past they shared and the future they desired. "Never let me go, Jeff, please, no matter what," she breathed.

Just then the phone rang, and Penny inhaled one sharp gulp. "I'll get it." Before it could sound a second time, she seized the receiver. Her knuckles white, the instrument shook in her grasp as she spoke. "Hello? Yes, this is Mrs. Baker."

"Isn't this peculiar?" Ellen turned to her companion. "No one seems to be home. What should I do, Dr. Stewart? I don't have a key."

"The first thing you should do is call me David. Then I think you should come with me to my house, which is not far away, and use the telephone. Perhaps one of your mother's friends will know where she is and when she'll be back."

"That's a great idea. I think that Nancy Hughes has a key, if all else fails. Do you know her?"

David picked up the suitcases. "As a matter of fact, I do. We can go by there to pick up the key if we can't find your mother. But first let's go to my house and make a pot of tea. Thank heavens you shipped most of your luggage. If the weight of these is any indication, your trunks will arrive by elephant express. I admit I'm not eager to carry your life's belongings all over Oakdale. What's in here anyway?"

"Just a few little pieces of the Blarney Stone.

Would you like some help, sir?"

Penny replaced the instrument in its cradle. After a moment she turned to Jeff and said brightly, "Silly me. That was just the doctor. My appointment has been changed to this afternoon. Would you drop me off on your way back to work?"

"Sure, honey, but is something wrong? You didn't tell me anything about an appointment." Jeff tried to keep his voice casual. The last thing he wanted to do was rock the boat.

She was ready at the stove, putting the finishing touches on their lunch. "You're such a worrywart. Of course there's nothing wrong. I'm just overdue for a checkup, that's all. That's all it is. Nothing more."

"But I thought you just had one a couple of months ago."

She kept her face to the stove, but he could see the color rising on the side of her neck. "This is a female-type check-up, Jeff."

"Oh."

Neither one of them spoke for several minutes. Jeff sat at the table leafing through *The Oakdale Gazette*, while his wife worked on the other side of the room.

Their lunchtime conversation was suddenly strained. Except for an occasional "please pass the milk" and "thank you," they didn't talk at all. When they were finished, they both looked at the clock and announced in unison, "Time to go." Then they broke into laughter which awkwardly dwindled a moment later.

"I'll get my coat," Penny said, "and I'll be with

you in a minute."

Jeff was waiting by the door when she returned. He opened it for her, stepped aside as she passed through, then closed it after himself. He strode rapidly to catch up to her, hoping to put his arm around her, but she kept several paces ahead of him all the way to the convertible.

"My, what a lovely home!" exclaimed Ellen. "So comfortable and friendly. Everything about it says that a wonderfully warm family must live here."

"Thank you. Betty did most of the designing, and we did a fair amount of the work ourselves. It did turn out rather well, if I must say so myself," he agreed proudly. "Please let me take your coat and then come and sit down and we'll have some coffee while we make our plans."

"Plans?" For the first time Ellen was thinking that it might not have been altogether wise to go with a stranger to his home.

"Yes, plans—for breaking and entering. We've got to figure out some way to get you into the Lowell mansion before nightfall. Suppose your mother is out of town, and suppose she took Nancy Hughes with her. We'll have to become cat burglars."

"Very funny," Ellen snorted. "I can see the headlines. Oakdale Police Nab Doctor and Debutante. At least my mother won't have to call up her friends to tell them I'm back."

"You were a debutante? Somehow I find that hard to believe." David shook with laughter.

"You've never heard of the Oakdale Cotillion?

That fabulous ball at which the fair young maidens of Oakdale's finest families are lined up and presented for all to admire? You haven't heard of it? Good, because it hasn't been thought of yet. Can you imagine anything more ghoulish?" Ellen glanced at him slyly. "No, I was never a debutante, though I must admit that when I was seventeen I thought it was very unfair that I couldn't be presented to society and have my pick of eligible husbands. I certainly got over that fast."

"Did you?"

"Yes, maybe too fast," she said. "Now how about that coffee? Let me help you make it. I don't think I trust you out of my sight. After breaking and entering, what's next?" She followed him into the kitchen ready to assist, then stood back in amusement as he handily produced coffeepot, cups, utensils, and even a tin of crackers.

"Yes, I can boil water," David remarked as he noticed her watching him intently.

She laughed gaily. "I'm just not used to seeing a man so at home in the kitchen," she explained. "My father practically never set foot in the place."

"Well, I've always been pretty competent around the house, and of course when my wife was sick, my skills came in quite handy. It was hard, I suppose, but then you never stop to think about much of anything else when you have a child depending on you."

"I guess you wouldn't," Ellen muttered vaguely as he busied himself at the stove, embarrassed at having spoken about such private matters to

106

someone he'd just met.

When they were done with their coffee, Ellen tried to locate her mother, but she couldn't. Finally she called Nancy Hughes. "Hello, Nancy, this is Ellen. Yes, I'm back in Oakdale. Thank you, I'm doing wonderfully, but I'm locked out, and I can't find my mother anywhere." After a pause, she said, "Oh, well, that explains it, doesn't it? Tell me, do you still have a key? Great, may I come over to pick it up? I'm at the Stewarts' house, Dr. David Stewart." She listened while Nancy asked her a question, then replied, "Just having coffee. He rescued me from the ordeal of having to take a taxi from the train station, and a good thing too. We'll be right over."

"So, what's the story?" David asked as he gathered up the dishes.

"She's out of town for a few days, and apparently my father is away on business. Nancy's got a key, though, so I'm not homeless. All I need is a ride over there. Knowing her as I do, I'm sure she'll insist I stay for dinner, so I won't be imposing on you any longer."

David seemed disappointed. "Believe me, it hasn't been an imposition. I enjoyed your company. Perhaps when Betty and the boys get back, you'll come and visit."

"That would be nice."

"Now if you'd just wait in the living room for a minute, I'll be right back. I've got to get a scarf from upstairs."

The Stewarts' home was so cozy and unpretentious, thought Ellen, so different from the house she had grown up in. What a perfect

AS THE WORLD TURNS

house for children, especially boys, she marveled
as she strolled into the living room. Spacious and
airy, it was a real family home. The handsome
doctor, his wife and two boys—they were the
realization of the American dream. This was a
dream that had eluded her till now, but she
hadn't given up hope. That, in a nutshell, was
the reason she had returned to Oakdale—to
reclaim what was rightfully hers.

Even the items on the mantelpiece made the
Stewarts appear to be the ideal family unit.
There were signed crayoned pictures showing
their creative development as well as their
varying interests. The older son, Paul, seemed to
be fascinated by machinery, judging from the
tractors and trucks he had drawn, while the
younger one was obviously interested in nature.
He drew trees, flowers, animals, and several
unidentifiable flying objects. Most of his work
looked as if it had been done with the aid of a
doting parent, patiently guiding a tiny hand over
the paper. What a happy little boy he must be,
she thought.

Next to the drawings and almost obscured by
them, was a glossy studio photograph of Dr. and
Mrs. Stewart on their wedding day, he good-
looking and proud, and she happy and glowing.
In a larger frame was a photo of Paul as a small
boy, taking what appeared to be his first steps as
his parents looked on with glee. Further down
the mantelpiece was a small picture of all four of
them at Christmastime, surrounded by gifts and
wrapping paper. And all the way at the end was a
simple snapshot of a little boy. Ellen didn't know
for sure who it was, so she picked it up and gazed

at it intently. After comparing it with the holiday photo, she decided it was obviously Danny. But there was something more, something compelling about the way that child looked, she felt. She held the picture up to the light and inspected it closely. She was right—she knew she was. There was something about that boy, something hauntingly familiar about his eyes that she couldn't escape.

"Tim!" she cried out in anguish.

"I beg your pardon," David said from the doorway. "Were you talking to me?"

Penny sat at the kitchen table and waited. It was time to tell Jeff the truth, time to stop the subterfuge. She needed his strength now more than ever. But the paramount question in her mind was whether or not he would be able to forgive her. In the whole year they had been married, Penny could not think of one other time she had lied to Jeff, even a little white lie. And this one was definitely not in the category of a little white lie. This was a big one, and she had no idea how he would react.

This lie involved Jeff—it involved their life together, all their hopes and dreams for the future. It was a devastating secret, and Penny couldn't keep it any longer. Why had she kept it from him? Why hadn't she just come out and told him the minute she had suspected what the problem was? It was probably the stupidest thing she had ever done, she confessed to herself. She deserved the suffering she was inflicting on herself. Was this the daughter of Chris and Nancy Hughes? She burst into tears at the thought. Where was the courage they had taught her? Where were the morals, the ethics?

"Where's my dinner?"

Penny looked up with a start. She hadn't even heard Jeff come in. "I haven't started it yet."

He looked at her blankly. "Why not?" He peeled off his coat and laid his hat and gloves on the counter. "Is something wrong?"

This was the moment of truth—Penny knew it was now or never. A tiny silent voice within her whispered, Never, never, but she ignored it. "Jeff," she began. "I've done something terrible. I have to talk to you about it."

He sat down with a thud, never taking his eyes off her. He watched her in silence. Finally he said, "Tell me! I don't care how bad it is, just spit it out. The suspense is killing me."

"Jeff, I . . . I . . . "

"Take a deep breath, dear, and then just tell me."

Penny inhaled, long and slow, and looked at him. "Jeff, I love you."

"Yes? Is that all?"

"Jeff, I love you more than I can say, and I have done something you may never forgive me for. I lied to you, honey, and I haven't been able to sleep ever since. Now my lie has caught up with me in a real bad way, and I have to tell you about it, even though it's too late." She took a quick breath, then continued. "Do you remember two weeks ago, when I told you I was going over to my mother's for the afternoon?"

Jeff's confused expression mirrored his words. "I have absolutely no idea what you're talking about."

"Of course you do," Penny persisted. "It was a Tuesday, and I had you drop me off there."

"All right, I remember. Now tell me what it has to do with anything."

"Well, I didn't go to my mother's."

"What?"

"I mean, I went there, but I didn't stay there. I went someplace else."

"Penny," he warned, "this is getting infuriating. Could you get to the point please?"

"Don't rush me, Jeff. You don't know how difficult this is for me." She stopped for another breath. "Now where was I?"

Jeff hooted in laughter. "What kind of joke is this? Tell me you're pulling my leg."

"Stop. This is not funny." Penny's voice was sharp with anxiety. "Believe me."

"Okay." Jeff struggled to keep a straight face.

Penny realized she had to take the plunge before she lost his attention completely. "That day," she said, "that you took me to my mother's, I went to the doctor's office, Jeff, for some tests. And today I went back for the results."

"What kind of tests?" Jeff quavered.

"The kind of tests you have when you want to start a family and nothing happens. You know how long we've been trying to have children, Jeff—it's been nearly a year. And I thought that something might be, you know, wrong, so I went to have it checked out. Actually my mother made me go."

"Nancy knows about this?" His voice rose and his face reddened.

"Jeff, don't get angry yet. Just hear me out. My

mother was right, much as I hate to admit it. I did need a checkup. And, Jeff, there is something wrong." She started to weep. "With me. There's something . . . I'm not . . . I can't . . . Jeff, if you want to leave me, I wouldn't blame you. In fact, I would understand completely. You deserve better than what I am."

"What? What? What?" Jeff fairly shrieked. "What are you talking about?"

The energy drained out of Penny before she could speak, and she slumped to the table. She lifted her chin to her hand and spoke dully, devoid of feeling. "The doctor told me I can never have children. I'm sterile. You'll never be a father with me as your wife, Jeff. You might as well just go. I'm not . . . I'm not really a complete woman. I'm nothing, Jeff. All my hopes are gone, all my dreams. All I ever wanted was to be your wife and to have your children and now I can't. And I never can."

Jeff said nothing. Slowly he got up from the table and put on his coat. He reached over to the counter and grabbed his hat and gloves. "I've gotta be alone," he barked. He slammed the door behind him and then he was gone.

Ellen wheeled around in utter distraction. "Who is this . . . this child?"

David joined her at the fireplace. "Why, that's Danny, our youngest. The little tyke—he wants so much to do everything his older brother can do. He was so funny about these pictures. The minute he saw Paul drawing, he wanted to make drawings too. The only problem is, he's not quite old enough to hold a pencil, much less draw with one. So Betty had to help him, but he got such a thrill out of it, you'd have thought he made every line himself and colored every leaf and every cow."

"Cow?"

David pointed to a brown blob. "What's the matter with you? Don't you recognize a cow when you see one? I tell you, that boy was proud, and Betty's so good with him. That little fellow changed our lives, and we bless the day we found him."

"What do you mean, found him?" Ellen dreaded the answer.

"Oh, didn't I tell you? Danny's adopted," David remarked with all the casualness he could bring to such a statement.

Ellen said nothing. She couldn't. The last thing she remembered was seeing David's smiling face growing smaller and smaller until finally it disappeared into blackness.

It was after midnight when Penny heard the turn of the key in the lock. She rolled over in bed, trying to look asleep, yet positioning herself so that she could have a clear view of the bedroom door. Moments later she saw him silhouetted in the light from the living room. He stood without moving, bracing himself against the door jamb, then softly called out, "Penny? I know you're awake. Please forgive me. I've been such a fool."

She sat up and held out her arms and he came to her. "Jeff, just tell me one thing. Do you still love me?"

His voice was low and trembling. "You bet I do. That took a lot of guts, what you did, and I got mad for all the wrong reasons. I got mad because I hadn't been there to help you when you needed me the most. I should have known. I'm your husband and I plan to be your husband for the rest of my life."

"But, Jeff, what about having children? You know it's something we've planned on and something we've looked forward to for years, even before we were married. What are we going to do now?"

Jeff fumbled for the words. "I don't really know. I mean, that's not the important thing any more, is it? What we should think about right now is you and your health, and how you feel about yourself. Not having children is an awful disappointment, and it must hurt you more than I could ever know. But, baby, we still have each other. I love you and you love me. Maybe it's terrible of me to say this, but how can it be the end of the world? When I look at you, I feel like I'm the luckiest man alive."

Penny snuggled deep into his arms. "With you by my side, I feel as if I can face anything. You're right, perhaps this is a tragedy, but it's going to take a lot more than this to ruin our happiness. Jeff, don't ever change. I want you always to be just as you are right now."

Chapter Eight
Love Found, Love Lost

Penny stood at the sink, waving goodbye out the kitchen window for what must have been the fourth time. She missed him so much when he was gone that she could hardly stand it. Ever since that horrible time all those weeks ago, she and Jeff had made a special effort to communicate. And it was really paying off. Their marriage was stronger than ever.

Knowing they'd never have any children together made them acutely aware of the many things they did have, and they rejoiced in their good fortune. It didn't really lessen the pain, but it certainly helped Penny put it in perspective.

Late one night Jeff remarked, "After all, it's not like we're two people who just decided to get married and that was that. We've had to fight for every bit of happiness we've gotten. I wouldn't dream of giving up something I've worked so hard for, and someone I want and need so much." He paused, then went on, "You know, we're not just an ordinary married couple in love." He smiled and touched Penny's hand. "You and I just happen to stand out in the crowd. We're unique,—and not just because we're the only twosome in Oakdale who drive a convertible in the dead of winter. Besides, now that I've started putting the top up, we're hardly noticeable at all. Believe me, it's not the car. It's something far more special, and it's something no one can ever take away from us."

Penny remembered being struck by the fact that he was both frivolous and deadly serious at the same time. It was almost as if he thought that if he didn't say what was on his mind right then, he'd never have another chance.

What a morbid idea, she realized, and she made an effort to shake it right out of her mind. Now she blew him one last kiss out across the morning sunshine, even though he was too far away to be able to see her. "I love you," she called, just as the thought hit her that she was the most nauseating newlywed she could think of, and their marriage was already a year old. Hmmph, she told herself, I hope I'm always this sickening.

She gathered up the breakfast dishes and slid them into the hot soapy water in the sink. Perhaps after she finished her housework, she'd give herself a little treat. She had wanted to do some redecorating, and today would be the perfect day to shop for new sheets and pillowcases for the bedroom. She might even find fabric for the curtains she had promised Jeff she would make. The only question was, who would go with her? This sort of expedition would be much more enjoyable if she had a friend to go with.

Without thinking, she dialed the first digits of her parents' number, then put her finger over the button. No, she realized delightedly, there's someone else I would really love to spend time with. Ellen is home, and Jeff and I have spent so much time together recently that I've barely seen her since she got back, she reminded herself.

The Lowells' number came back to her in a flash, and her fingers nimbly spun around the dial. This will be fun, she told herself, because we have so much to catch up on. If we get tired of discussing Ellen's trip to Europe or my newfound happiness with Jeff, then I could bring Ellen up to date on everything that had gone on in Oakdale in the past year or so.

The phone rang and rang. How strange, Penny thought. It's awfully early for everyone to be out.

Ellen sat stiffly on the cold, hard-backed chair in the courtroom. Distractedly she twisted her hands in her lap and rubbed her fingers back and forth, trying to induce some warmth into the joints. She couldn't help but notice the bareness of her hands. The day after Tim's funeral, she'd taken off her rings, and she could not bring herself to put them back on. She didn't want to feel phony. Not at a time like this.

She wished that her mother would hurry with the coffee. Mornings were difficult as it was, but this waiting was intolerable. She had prepared herself for this for months, and ever since she'd begun the proceedings, she had tried to gather her strength for the time she would be facing very soon now. Yet deep within herself, she harbored a secret doubt. Was she doing the right thing? Just because it was what she wanted, did that mean it was good for everyone concerned?

Perhaps she had started too soon, but try as she might, she could not hold herself back. She hadn't always been that way, she knew. As a youngster, before all this had happened, she'd always considered the other person first. Whatever she had done, she had first considered its effect on others and had tried to predict their reactions. But now she was functioning differently. She had spent so much energy looking into her own mind and heart that it was impossible for her to ignore what she had found there. If only she could find some concrete assurance that she was doing the right thing.

Slowly the room began to fill up, and Ellen's mind crowded with remembrances of the last few years. She wondered if people could read her thoughts, if anyone really knew what she was going through. She decided she didn't care. Soon after Tim was so cruelly taken from her, she forced herself to accept the fact that she would have to go through this alone. Even her parents weren't able to help her that much, though she had to admit that she appreciated them putting their own difficulties on the back burner in order to stand beside her when she needed them so much.

It had all begun when she'd first met Tim in between classes at college. He had been Dr. Cole to her then, and as a part-time member of the science faculty, he had been someone she looked up to, even idolized. Eventually this hero-worship had turned to love, and Tim had felt the same way. By then there had been no turning back. Even the obstacle of his marriage had seemed inconsequential. To Tim it had been a minor annoyance, and to Ellen it had been a tantalizing reminder that she now had a sure-fire way of getting even with her father for all the years of misery and embarrassment he had caused. But before she'd had a chance to rub his nose in it, everything had changed. The day she'd discovered she was pregnant was the day her life had taken a whole new turn that she had never planned on.

Then when Tim had declared his true and lasting love for her, and had proven it by divorcing his wife and marrying her, she'd finally believed that she could regain her lost direction. By then it had been too late—too late for Ellen, too late for Tim, too late for the child they had created together. And by now, she knew, it was also too late for regrets.

"Goodness, you're a million miles away! Here's your coffee, dear." Claire sounded unnaturally cheerful above the growing hubbub.

"Thanks, Mom. What took you so long? I missed you. You know, I thought I was ready for this, but now I'm not so sure. If everyone would quit staring at me, I'd feel more comfortable."

"No one is staring at you, dear," Claire reassured her, "and the only people here are those who are directly involved. There is no way this is going to be easy, but I want you to know that I'm behind you no matter what happens."

"Don't say that!" Ellen ordered with ferocity. "There is only one way this can turn out, and I won't let anything else happen. Is that clear?"

The room suddenly fell silent. Ellen shrank back in her chair, certain every eye was upon her. The gavel sounded, and each hair on her head seemed to stand on end as she heard the words she had anticipated for so long.

"All rise. Court is now is session," the clerk intoned, "in the matter of the custody of the minor child Daniel Stewart. Are all parties present?"

The sunlight glinted off the pavement as Jeff checked the road ahead for an opportunity to pass. Better hustle, he told himself. He hadn't left on time and he didn't want to be late getting back from lunch. He just hoped Penny would have everything all ready by the time he got there.

Ah, there, he thought triumphantly, there's a spot. He downshifted briskly, popped the clutch out, and jammed down on the accelerator. The convertible leapt forward, and he speedily threaded his way around the car in front of him.

This new lunchtime ritual they had adopted was something he had begun to look forward to. He'd first suggested it to Penny in the hope that it would cheer her up, and also give him a chance to check on her moods. When the doctor had first told her she was unable to bear children, she had taken it very hard, but with his help she had managed to pull through. Still he'd wanted to keep a careful eye on her because he knew only too well just how fragile she could be.

At last, though, she seemed to be finding other interests, and she seemed, on the surface at least, to be putting this behind her. Jeff knew that he deserved a lot of the credit for this. Penny had certainly made the change, but he had been the catalyst. Somehow the right words had come to him, though it was still a mystery how he'd done it, how he'd been able to guide her to a deeper understanding of her feelings. He'd managed to express his own feelings in a way that really reached her. In fact, the night that he had broken down and cried out his sorrow and bitterness at her sterility was the night that she had finally begun to accept it. They had held each other all night long, two bodies in the darkness, racked by sobs. Then by the light of dawn they had made the sweetest love imaginable and felt they had started their life anew.

Jeff smiled. Why had no one ever told him that being with a woman could be like that? Whatever masculine sex talk he had ever heard had never touched on the caring, sensitive aspect of love. Until he had met Penny, Jeff had believed that men and women were just totally different, romantically speaking. Now all that had changed. As Penny and Jeff developed their marital relationship, passion and romance had become part of each other. Together they had become adults, capable of experiencing and expressing a far wider range of emotions than they had ever been aware of before.

When he held her in his arms, he could feel her body melt against his, as if they were truly one. And when she looked at him, her gaze penetrated to his very soul. She understood him so completely that with her, he was totally himself.

Not that he forgot about the physical side of love. By no means. Penny excited him more than ever, and he could sense that he had an equally strong effect on her. She often teased him about his good looks, yet when she spoke of his firm muscles and fine body, she seemed somehow proud that they were hers alone to enjoy. And as for him, he loved the clean, sweet smell of her soft hair, and the few tiny freckles on her shoulders drove him wild. Each curve of her body was a marvel to him.

Keep your mind on the road, he reminded himself, as he gripped the steering wheel resolutely. He scanned the highway for another chance to pass, and shortly it came. Again he shifted into second and moved out into the other lane. It was a long straightaway with no traffic, so he took his time. Leisurely he shifted back into high gear and moved past a tiny sports car, then alongside a pickup full of bales of hay. The wind blew through his hair and invigorated his scalp. His cheeks flushed and he took in air in deep energizing gulps.

Up the road a few hundred feet, he could see that the warm mid-day sun had melted the snowbank by the side of the road, and the pavement shimmered with a thin sheen of water on it. The deep azure blue of the sky reflected brilliantly off the water's surface, and its beauty momentarily brought his thoughts back to Penny and the hypnotic intensity of her eyes. In their bottomless pools he saw love, faith, and commitment. When she looked at him that way, he felt truly alive and loved.

Within seconds the wheels of his car were

skimming the water, sending up tiny droplets into the air. He moved the steering wheel slightly to the right to regain his position in his lane, but there was no reaction from his car. He moved it harder. Still no response. Simultaneously letting up on the accelerator, he cranked it hard and felt the tail lurch forward as his car began a violent spin. Next he heard a thunderous crash, and his final recollection was of catapulting up through the air. For one brief but everlasting second, he felt free as a bird. Then the earth rushed up to meet him and he felt nothing.

Penny sat on the edge of her seat in the Lowells' living room, or the front parlor, as they called it. Ellen's story was so incredible, that Penny was having a hard time assimilating it. And so far Ellen had barely scratched the surface. Penny considered her own life to be chock full of drama, but even the most cataclysmic events she'd experienced seemed pale compared to what her friend was going through now. She had known about the pregnancy, of course, and the subsequent adoption of the infant, but she had never even considered that the baby might be living right here in Oakdale. She'd certainly had no clue that when Ellen had returned from Europe so suddenly, it had been for one overpowering reason—to gain custody of the baby she'd given away.

Before her was an Ellen Lowell she barely knew. As a girl, Ellen had been a follower, not a leader. But the narrator of this tale of lost hopes and renewed desires was a woman of courage and character. In her youth she had been given every material possession possible, yet she'd lacked the one thing every child needs. She had never had security. She'd never known from one minute to the next what to expect from her parents, and many people of lesser mettle would have buckled under the strain. Yet Ellen appeared to have thrived, despite a string of personal disasters. The security she'd so desperately craved she'd found within herself. It was from that well of self-belief that she now drew the courage she needed to see her through this latest of her trials.

"A custody battle is an ugly thing," she was saying, "but I know I can never live with myself unless I try to get my son back. And I vowed to myself that this was one thing I'd never do halfway. I swore I wouldn't undertake it until I was ready to see it through to the finish. Penny, if you could only understand how hard it was for me to give up my son before I ever even had a chance to hold him, then you would see that by comparison this is easy for me now.

"At the time I thought I was doing the right thing for the baby, but what I never allowed myself to consider was what I wanted. Somehow I needed to punish myself for my affair with Tim, and the handiest and most complete way of doing that was to deny myself the right to raise our child. Then after he died, I realized that so much of life is wrenched away from us against our will, that it makes no sense at all to abandon a very real part of ourselves. I can be a good mother to Danny. He is my son, and I want him. He belongs with me, and I intend to see to it that he grows up with his mother. Heaven knows, he'll never have a chance to know his father, and

I can't allow myself to keep him from his own mother any longer."

Penny gaped at her friend in admiration and disbelief. "I don't know if I ever could be as strong as you. You have such deep conviction that what you're doing is right, and I don't know if I'll ever have that for myself. I'm such a little cry-baby sometimes. Fortunately I have Jeff to help me through the rough spots." Suddenly she turned stark white. "Jeff!" she gasped. "Oh, my God, Jeff!"

"For goodness sakes, what's wrong?" Ellen asked.

Penny was gripped by an inexplicable confusion. "Jeff . . ." she faltered, "Jeff comes home for lunch. He comes home every day. And I'm always there for him, always. Today I missed it. It slipped my mind completely. It's one-thirty already, and I never even thought of it, not once. Why, Ellen, why?"

Ellen's reply was cut off by the insistent ring of the doorbell. She rushed to the front hall, Penny at her heels, and opened the door.

"Excuse me, I've just got to go." Penny grabbed her coat and darted down the steps, leaving Ellen quite speechless.

Her visitor shifted his weight uncomfortably, until at last she spoke. "Won't you come in please, Dr. Stewart?"

It was nightfall before Chris and Nancy could convince their daughter to leave the hospital. Jeff's body had long since been removed to the funeral home, and there was no purpose in staying anywhere near the emergency room.

Penny had been rambling incoherently, and they had tried every trick they knew to get her to come home with them. Finally they had simply taken her bodily, Nancy on one arm and Chris on the other, and had put her into the car. They all sat in the front seat, which was usually a little crowded for three. But Penny was huddled up into such a tiny ball between them, it seemed as if they were transporting a small, helpless child.

Now she was home, curled up on the sofa in the Hughes' living room, clutching a throw pillow and talking to her dead husband. "Where did you go, Jeff?" she cried. "Where are you? Why did you leave me? Why now? What about all the babies we were going to have, Jeff? Why did you leave before our babies were born?"

To Nancy this was beyond heartbreaking, but she knew there was nothing she could do. Once the shock wore off, Penny's mind would return to normal. True, she was fragile, and she had nearly snapped once before, but Nancy felt with a mother's intuition that her daughter would survive this latest cruel blow. Denial is a natural way of dealing with death, she told herself, though she had to admit that all this talk of babies was downright creepy. She had thought that Penny had finally made her peace with that issue, but apparently this latest trauma had reawakened Penny's desire for children.

"Let me take you upstairs to bed, darling. I know you need to lie down," she said soothingly.

"Carry me," her daughter commanded in a voice she had not heard from her in many, many years.

"Just take my hand and I'll help you," Nancy

said, as tears coursed down her cheeks. "I'm by your side, and I always will be. It may not seem so now, but there will be an end to your pain. You will start life anew once again when you're ready, and I'll be there with you to do anything you need. Only please, please let me help you."

Ellen was exhausted. David had been talking to her for nearly six hours, and her resistance was wearing thin. One point he'd made over and over again kept sticking in her mind, and that was that they both had an obligation to do what was best for Danny—without regard for what either of them might want. True, Betty's health had suffered terribly as a result of the custody battle, and she continued to deteriorate. David's work at the hospital had been riddled with errors lately, as he'd found himself completely unable to concentrate. And Ellen had been unable to find meaning in anything unless she first found assurance that she would regain her son.

"But none of that has anything to do with Danny," David insisted for the umpteenth time. "The only thing we should be talking about here is what's best for him. Already the stress in our household is affecting him, though thank heavens, he's too young to have any idea what it's all about. He's usually such a happy little boy, toddling around after his big brother and getting into mischief like little boys do. But now he sits a lot because Paul is too worried to play with him much, and Betty is so preoccupied that she can't even see straight. I understand how you feel, Ellen, honestly I do, but if you could see what this is doing to that little fella, you'd give up and never look back. He has a right to a happy and secure life, and he's found it in our home. I don't think it's good for him that you're trying to take all that away from him."

"I'm not trying to rob him of his chance for happiness. I swear I'm not," Ellen protested weakly, "but he is my flesh and blood. I don't know if I can live with the agony of not having him with me. I just don't know."

"Please, Ellen, I beg you, you must try. Not for my sake or for Betty's, but for your son's. To be uprooted at a time like this could be devastating for him, and I love him so much, I can't bear the thought of him being hurt. Now he has a complete family, a mother and a father and a brother even, and you can't offer him that. You're a single woman, Ellen, and society doesn't look kindly on women who have children out of wedlock, or who give them up for adoption. Most people would feel that you gave up all your rights to him when you first gave him away."

"Do you feel that way?" Ellen had no idea why his opinion was so important to her.

"No, I don't. I know you to be a fine person, and I can't put a label on you. But other people will, and even if you win this case, your life afterwards is going to be very difficult. Every obstacle you find will be magnified in impact for Danny. I can't emphasize it enough—I don't want to see him hurt."

Ellen knew what she must do. She must call on all her reserves of strength for this latest undertaking—she must redouble her efforts on Danny's behalf. But she must redirect them as well. As intolerable as it had been to give him up when he was first born, it was insignificant compared to the pain she was about to inflict on herself. To forsake him a second time would give her torment she couldn't even begin to imagine, but she knew she had no choice. To be confronted on one hand with hurting her son and on the other hand with hurting herself, was really no choice at all. The answer was obvious to her at last. She thanked God that her deep strength eased at least the pain of the decision.

"Yes, David," she said, "I can't see Danny hurt either. The whole procedure is started, but I'll end it. I'll walk into court tomorrow morning and drop my request for custody."

Chapter Nine
Death Struggle

Danny toddled through the kitchen, wavered slightly in the dining room doorway, then made a beeline for the living room sofa, where Ellen was seated. He clambered up onto the cushions, then plopped himself squarely in her lap. Grasping her chin between his two tiny fists, he brought her face close to his. "Park," he announced determinedly. "Wanna play at park."

In love and wonder, Ellen looked at him, then turned her face away as she felt her eyes brim over with tears. There was so much she wanted to say to him, yet so little she could let him know.

"Okay," she covered brightly, "the park is fine. But you must wear a sweater. The weather is starting to get cold. And bring a bag. We'll gather colored leaves on the way over. Then when we come back here, perhaps we can make some harvest decorations. Do you know what those are?"

"No. Wanta play with my truck. Can I?"

"Of course you can, sweetheart. You can do anything you like. I'm just glad that I can spend time with you today."

Danny put his arms around her and gave her a kiss. "I like you. You play with me. You take me to the park." His little face shone with delight.

Frannie Brennan, the Stewarts' housekeeper, strode into the room. "All right, young man, that will do. You've bothered Miss Lowell quite enough for one day. I'm sure she has better things to do than make mud pies in the park with you. Now, march, because it's time for me to give your face a good scrubbing, and then I think you should lie down for a while."

Danny clung to Ellen. "No," he said stubbornly. "Park."

"Frannie, don't you think it would be good for him to get some outdoor exercise?" Ellen controlled herself with difficulty. Somehow Frannie always managed to rub her the wrong way. "Sweetheart, you run along while I talk to Mrs. Brennan about this. Perhaps you could look in the mirror and see whether you think your face needs to be cleaned. Is there anything else you can think of that might need a little cleaning up?"

Danny looked puzzled for a moment, then inspected his hands. "These?" He held up two very grubby little paws.

Ellen laughed. "Good thinking. Now go do something about it, and then we'll go outside."

"Okay," he chirped happily, as he scampered out of the room.

Frannie fixed an angry stare on Ellen. "You certainly know very little about child-rearing, and I'll thank you to leave his care to me. Danny is too young to be capable of washing his hands properly, as well as many other things, and I've been hired to see to it that he receives the right kind of guidance and control."

"We differ very much on what we consider best for Danny, don't we? But somehow I don't think that's the problem here. Would you like to talk about it while my son is out of the room?" Ellen challenged.

"I don't know what you mean. I've given you every opportunity to be a friend to Danny and I've never tried to make you feel unwelcome here. And how have I been repaid for my kindness? You come in here ready to take over Danny's life before poor Mrs. Stewart is even cold in her grave. Furthermore, you have the nerve to act sorry she died, when you yourself are the main cause that unfortunate woman passed away. So please don't come to me acting pious. Her death was just the opportunity you were waiting for."

Ellen took a deep breath. "Perhaps this isn't the right time to discuss this, after all. Any kind of tension that affects Danny is really a matter for Dr. Stewart to deal with, don't you think?"

The housekeeper's face hardened at the mention of David's name. "How dare you threaten—" she began, then broke off as Danny entered the room. Her face dark with fury, she spun on her heel and stalked out.

"Ready for the park?" Ellen asked the boy.

"Ready, set, go!" he shouted as he raced for the door.

"Just a second. What about that sweater I mentioned? Come on, let's go upstairs and find one." She gathered him up in her arms and gave him a kiss. Frannie Brennan be damned, she thought. I love this boy.

Don and Penny were sitting in their favorite spot in the whole house, the kitchen table. In front of them were two cups of coffee, untouched, and a plate of sweet rolls, still in the same neat arrangement Nancy had left.

"I came home to see how you were doing, and all I seem to be doing is talking about myself and my own problems." Don chuckled ruefully and reached across the table to run his fingers down the side of his sister's cheek. "So tell me, how are you?"

Penny looked up at him with red-rimmed eyes. "Oh, Don," she moaned, "it's been six months already and I still can't get over it. Why does the pain last so long? Am I going to weep for him longer than I loved him?"

"I know it must seem like that, but it's something you have to go through, that's all. If grief were understandable and rational, then it wouldn't work on us the way it does. It's mysterious, it's awful, it feels like it's never going to end. But I guarantee you that when it does end, you will feel better. This is just your way of saying how much you really loved Jeff, and there is no way it's going to be easy." He touched her arm. "Am I making any sense at all?"

She sighed and looked away, then turned back to him. "I suppose you are, but I just don't want to admit it. I loved him more than anything in my life, and we went through so much to be together, and then we had only moments together before he was gone. Now I know I should be grateful for the time we had—heaven knows I've been told I should—but it doesn't seem fair that we should only have had moments. Why couldn't we have had a lifetime? Why do I have to be left here feeling like this?"

"You don't, Penny, you don't," Don comforted. "You just have to deal with your feelings, and then they won't seem so overwhelming. Now this may seem like a terribly insensitive question, but I want you to think about it anyway. What is absolutely the worst thing about having Jeff gone?"

Penny reacted as if she'd been slapped. She pushed her chair back, stood up, and started out of the room. But before she could get more than several steps, her brother had caught up with her. Firmly he put his arms around her and led her back to her chair.

"I'm sorry. I just thought that if you could talk about whatever the worst pain was, then maybe the rest of it wouldn't be so bad." Don's voice was understanding, but not apologetic.

Penny cradled her chin in her hands, and the dullness of her eyes slowly grew to a deep piercing stare that took her back many months. She looked as if she would cry, but when she spoke, she sounded almost like her old self. "The really bad thing, the worst, most painful thing of all, Don, is that I'm not sure Jeff knew how much I loved him. I know I told him and I know I was a good wife, but I don't know if I showed him in a way he really could grasp. You know, you always think, well, there's tomorrow, I'll show him tomorrow. I'm sure I did that. I held love back from him because I counted on there always being a tomorrow. And there isn't. Damn it, there isn't! All we have is today, and we can't waste it!" Penny's vehemence surprised even herself, and she fell quiet.

Don hesitated a long minute before he broke the silence. His voice barely above a whisper, he said, "That's right. That's it. All we have is today. Regrets for the past are as useless as fears of the future. Why have we both had such a hard time learning that?"

"Because, my dear brother, we've never fully accepted the fact that we're not in control of the universe," Penny retorted smartly. "It's always been a shock to our systems when we aren't able to get other people or the world to give us exactly what we want."

"How did you get so clever all of a sudden? I'm supposed to be the one giving the advice around here. Instead it seems like you're analyzing me," Don bantered.

"If the shoe fits . . . Seriously, though, I don't mean to make light of your problems with Ellen. The way that's turning out must be every bit as hurtful as the way my life with Jeff ended. At least he never fell in love with someone else. I don't know how you stand it. And now to hear that she and Dr. Stewart are planning to be married—well, that must be more than you can bear. You were there for her when she needed a shoulder to lean on and —"

"That's all I was for her—a shoulder to lean on. But just because I wanted more from her doesn't mean I had any right to expect it. She's not a bad person, or even a selfish one. She's a fine woman, but she isn't the woman for me. Now if I could only accept that, I could get on with my life. I guess what it comes down to is being man enough to accept my own good advice."

"You are, Don, believe me. You're just about the best man I know. And somewhere you'll find the right woman for you—don't you ever doubt it."

"Yeah, I guess." Don cleared his throat, embarrassed by his emotions. "Now how about us having some hot coffee? This stuff is ice cold."

Ellen sat on the bench beside the sandbox, watching Danny and his two little friends furiously digging sand out of one hole, then trucking it over to fill another. Occasionally the boys disagreed over whose turn it was for the shovel or the truck, but Ellen sat on the sidelines. Only if there was the actual threat of toddler violence would she intervene. Otherwise her attitude was that they should work it out themselves. Cooperation was one of the main lessons of the playground, and though she took care to remind Danny of it on the walk over, and to congratulate him about it on the way home, while he was at play, he was on his own. Experience is the best teacher, she told herself, and from it she'd learned more than just a lesson or two in her lifetime. As frustrating as it was to give freedom to a son she had only just met, she knew with all her heart that it was the only way he would grow up strong and sure of himself.

"Is this the way you supervise him? Look at that. He's making a mess!"

"Frannie, what are you doing here?" Ellen

looked up in shock.

"I decided I had a few things to say to you that couldn't wait. Do you want me to start right here and now, or shall we step out of earshot?"

Ellen had never heard her speak so insolently. Frannie seemed well on her way to a boiling rage. Quickly she stepped away from the sandbox and walked briskly to a spot near a scrubby pine tree from which she could still see Danny. She turned to face her adversary. Forcefully she stated, "This is neither the time nor the place for this. I suggest you get yourself under control, and we'll talk about this another time."

"Now! I will talk now, and you will listen!" Frannie's eyes were taking on a demoniac glare, and she shook her finger in Ellen's face as she spoke. "First of all, I won't let you marry David. You tricked him into asking you, and he doesn't know what he wants. I'm not about to let him make a mistake he'll regret for the rest of his life. For the past year, ever since his wife died, I've taken care of him, and he belongs to me. He's mine, not yours, and I won't let you have him!"

"Shouldn't David have some say in this?" Ellen inquired mildly, struggling to keep the situation from getting out of hand.

"Don't you even speak about him!" she shrieked, and several mothers turned in horror to see what was going on. "You're not worthy of even breathing his name! You're not fit to be a mother to his children, and I'll never let you take my place in their hearts. I don't want you to come near them and I don't want you to come near David—do you understand me?" Her voice had risen to an hysterical pitch, and Ellen could sense that everyone in the playground was staring at them. Danny had stopped playing and was running over to see what was wrong.

Frannie leaned in to Ellen and whispered her final threat. "If you don't do as I say, I'll tell that little boy that you're the mother who abandoned him years ago, and he'll hate you forever. Now you just think about that!"

Ellen reeled in shock. Danny was her one weak point. There was nothing anyone could do to her that could hurt her anymore, but Danny was another matter. For two years he had known little but turmoil and loss, and she could not bring herself to add to it. When would this end? Would she have to give him up yet another time to ensure him a life of happiness?

Frannie took Danny's hand in triumph. "We're going home. Don't follow us."

Ellen nodded dumbly. Heartbroken, she watched her little son look over his shoulder and blow her a kiss. Then with one last yank from the housekeeper, he disappeared from her sight.

Ellen was in quandary. For hours she sat in the park, searching for a way out of the situation. None of the options appealed to her at all. If she went to David about this and forced Frannie to carry through her threat, the harm to Danny would last his whole life long. But if she kept silent, then she would not only lose her son, but also her future husband. Whatever she chose, she would lose.

For the past two years, Danny's welfare had been the only basis for all her decisions. Twice before she had given him up, and she wasn't sure she could do it again. Besides, this time she couldn't convince herself that it was in his best interests. For one thing, she didn't believe Frannie's influence on her son was even remotely healthy. Secondly, Ellen could feel that Danny loved her, and there was simply no reason other than Frannie's threat to deprive Danny of her love.

The more Ellen thought about it, the more she realized that Frannie was using Danny because she desperately wanted to become the next Mrs. David Stewart. That really was the basic issue, Ellen realized in amazement. Frannie was in love with David, but she could not deal with it rationally. That explained so many peculiar incidents, including Frannie's near-hysteria at Betty's funeral, and her attacks on Ellen afterward. Betty had died of coronary failure, and the weakness of her heart stemmed from a childhood case of rheumatic fever rather than anything Ellen had done. If anyone had benefited by Betty's death, it most surely had been Frannie.

All through Betty's illness and then after her death, Frannie had consolidated her power and influence at the Stewart home. She'd tried to assume full control over the children's upbringing, and she'd been very upset when David had turned to Ellen for advice and help with the boys. Then when David and Ellen had fallen in love, she'd become more desperate. For a long time Ellen hadn't realized that Frannie intentionally altered messages she had left for David, and that she often hadn't told him when Ellen had called at all. When she had first discovered Frannie's treachery, she had figured it was simple jealousy and had worked around it. But now it had gotten completely out of hand.

This was blackmail. There were no two ways about it. If Ellen didn't do what Frannie wanted, then Frannie would destroy Danny's happiness. The more Ellen considered the dilemma she was in, the angrier she became. This was between her and Frannie, and Danny was merely an innocent victim.

It all was becoming crystal clear to her now. As soon as she and David had announced their engagement, Frannie became very hostile. Now Ellen understood why it never occurred in front of David. The one time she'd mentioned Frannie's conduct, David had belittled her concern, saying, "Frannie always speaks so highly of you, yet you seem to bear some sort of grudge against her."

She really had been played for a fool, and it was time to end this game once and for all. Her mind was made up. She would confront Frannie, but she'd wait to do it until David could be there. To do it alone would be unwise, even unsafe.

Stiffly she got to her feet and stretched her limbs. She'd been sitting in one position for so long that every muscle in her body ached. She decided she would walk back to the Stewart house, and if David was there, she would go inside. Otherwise, she would sit in her car and wait for him to arrive home.

She felt that she could defeat Frannie with the truth, but she still dreaded each and every step that took her closer to the fiendish housekeeper. In the waning light, trees and bushes along the sidewalk took on an eerie glow as, one by one, lights winked on in the homes she passed. The air grew chill, and Ellen shivered slightly. She wasn't looking forward to this one bit, and she sighed with relief when she noticed that the Stewarts' driveway was empty. David wasn't home yet, thank heavens, so she could just wait outside.

When she got near her car, she reached into her pocket for the keys, and with dismay, she remembered that she'd left them inside on the coffee table in the living room. Well, she would just have to go in and get them, even if it meant facing Frannie. Surely with both boys home, Frannie would be able to control herself. In any case, it was a chance she would just have to take. She couldn't wait all night on the street.

As she walked up the steps to the front door, the porch light flashed on and the door was flung open. There Frannie stood, hands on her hips, her face glittering with hatred. "I thought I told you never to show your face near here again. Now get out of my sight!"

"I'm here for my car keys. If you'll just move aside, I'll come in and get them, and then I'll be on my way." Clearly this was not the time for any type of discussion with Frannie, Ellen decided. The woman was obviously too overwrought already. She brushed past her and made her way to the living room as Frannie slammed the front door behind her.

"Now that I've got you here, there are a few things I'd like to add to what I told you this afternoon," the housekeeper muttered as she advanced menacingly toward Ellen. "The first thing I've decided is that you should leave Oakdale."

"Leave Oakdale!" sputtered Ellen. "That's absurd. I have no intention of doing something so ridiculous just because you tell me to."

"You'll do exactly as I say or I'll see to it that you never see your son again, and that you never see your beloved Dr. Stewart again either," the woman ranted on.

I must get out of here, Ellen realized with growing panic. She's really unhinged, far madder than I ever thought. If David doesn't come home or if I can't get out the door soon, this situation will get completely out of control.

As if she had read her mind, Frannie smiled victoriously as she told her, "You'd better not wait for your white knight to rescue you. Dr. Stewart took the boys out to dinner, and they won't be home for hours. I have you all to myself. First of all, as I said, you're to leave Oakdale. Obviously I can't trust you to stay away from him, so you must move away. You're to forget all about your little boy, and heaven knows that shouldn't be too difficult for you. You've abandoned him twice before. You should be used to it by now. Only this time, you're to forget about him permanently. No letters, no phone calls, no contact of any kind. That way you won't have any reason to have anything to do with Dr. Stewart, and I can get on with my life as I've planned. Once you're removed, everything will be perfect."

Ellen fought the urge to reply. There was so much she wanted to say, but she knew that anything she said would only infuriate Frannie.

"Let me by," she insisted. "I want to leave."

"No. Now that you're here, you'll stay here until you agree to what I say. Now sit." Frannie stuck out a long bony arm and shoved Ellen backward into an armchair.

Ellen caught herself with her hand and struggled to sit upright. The housekeeper loomed over and began to laugh. It was a strange laugh, and it frightened Ellen. She had always felt uncomfortable around Frannie, but she had never imagined that Frannie had the potential for madness. All she could think about was escape. She pushed herself up out of the chair and snatched her keys from the table before Frannie could get to her. But when she tried to wriggle past her, Frannie grabbed her by the hair and hurled her to the floor.

Ellen howled as much from pain as from abject terror. The woman's strength was almost superhuman. She looked up just in time to see Frannie grab a lamp from the table and throw it at her. Quickly she rolled, covering her face as glass shattered just a few inches from her.

She pulled herself to her feet and huddled behind the armchair, frantically hunting for a way past the raving woman and out of the room. Keeping her eyes locked on Frannie's, she cautiously inched away from the chair and toward the security of the sofa. Just when she reached it, Frannie picked up the poker from the fireplace and wielded it. Ellen ducked as it whistled over her head, then darted to the side as Frannie took another swing. Ellen tried to snatch the poker as it went by, in a vain attempt to wrench it from her, but it slipped from her grasp. In desperation she plucked a small table from her path and threw it at Frannie's feet. The housekeeper lunged for her, but as she did so, she tangled her feet on the table and fell with a sickening thud.

Ellen ran for the door, then looked back to see if Frannie was following her. But the housekeeper lay where she had fallen, sprawled on the floor with the poker at her side. Ellen tiptoed up to her to see if she was really unconscious, and then she saw the blood slowly trickling from her mouth. The woman didn't move, and in horror Ellen realized she must be dead.

"I've killed her!" she cried, just as the front door flew open. Standing there were a man and woman Ellen dimly recognized as being next-door neighbors.

"Call the police, Henry," ordered the woman. "Tell them we've witnessed a murder."

Chapter Ten
So Many Prisons

Penny tried to force the gaiety from her face. It shouldn't have been hard, considering her grim surroundings. But she had been miserable for so long that she was unwilling to forego her happiness even for a few minutes. Especially now that it was spring, nature's time of rebirth.

It had been such hard work to recover from Jeff's death. Together they'd had such high hopes for their marriage and had handled so many bitter disappointments. Alone Penny hadn't known whether or not she had the stamina to deal with the heartache. At first she had believed that Jeff's tenacity had seen them through their annulment and his murder trial, and then more recently, her sterility. Heaven knows, she had let each of those crises throw her into a tailspin, and each time her strong husband had rescued her from the brink of mental collapse. So after the accident, she had fully expected to hit the skids. True, for a while there it had been touch-and-go, but in the end she had regained her emotional health.

She remembered that first day she'd left her parents' house and had gone for a walk. After weeks and weeks of remaining in her room, she had awakened one morning and heard birds singing outside her window. It seemed almost silly to her now, but she'd felt as if she'd never heard such beautiful sounds before. Stealthily she'd left her room and gone downstairs and had made it out the front door without alerting anyone that she'd left. Briefly she had considered waking Don up for company, but the poor man had put his own problems aside so many times to listen to her, and so many times he had thought she'd been on the road to recovery. But each time she had slipped back into the deepest despondency. This time at least, she would spare him any possible disappointment and keep her fragile and newfound hopes a secret until she was sure they would stay with her.

Sure enough, by the time she returned from her walk, she felt positively reborn. So many things Jeff had said to her during his short lifetime came back to her, not as haunting reminders, but as everlasting truths for her to live by.

It was then that she first began to consider what Jeff would have wanted her to do with her life. Would he want her to pine away in remembrance and regret? Or would he encourage her to go after life with the vigor and appreciation he'd always had? As soon as she even began to ask herself the question, she knew the answer.

From there on it hadn't exactly been easy, but Penny had to admit it hadn't been so traumatic either. When she finally met Neil, she was ready for a relationship with a man, and she was prepared to evaluate him on his own merits, not as a replacement for the husband she'd lost.

This was not to say that she hadn't compared them endlessly at first, or that even now she didn't stop at times to ponder how Jeff would have said something or done something in a different way. And there was no avoiding it— there were some very basic differences between her feelings for Neil and those she'd once had for Jeff. Love with Neil was comforting, sweet, lasting, and mature. With Jeff it had been unpredictable, thrilling, even a bit naughty.

Sometimes late at night she missed Jeff desperately, and then she would look over at Neil lying there so serenely beside her, and she would wonder if it was ever possible to have everything she wanted at once. When morning came, she knew that the security she had found in her marriage to Neil would give her the strength to cope with anything that might happen to her. She thanked God that so far nothing had. The few months they'd been married had been a time of peace and solace for her. She was rebuilding her life, and at the same time they were forging their lives together. For the first time in her life she could look to the future with no fear whatsoever. Even with Jeff there had always been some nagging doubt, however small, that occasionally troubled her. But now she faced adulthood and responsibility with joy and faith, and she recognized that much of her inner stability she owed to Neil.

A contented smile broke out on her face as she thought of his gentleness, his honesty, and his solid belief in himself. He had so many all-American virtues that it almost embarrassed her to be married to him. Many of her friends thought he would make the perfect husband, but since he truly was near-perfect, she knew that none of them would ever have a chance with him.

One afternoon at the bookstore a woman had made a really blatant pass at him. Instead of asserting his masculinity by teasing back, he had blushingly informed the woman that he was happily attached to a lovely woman whom he loved beyond words. Penny had walked in from the back room just at the moment of truth, and the humiliated customer had actually apologized before scurrying out the door. She and Neil had laughed for days about that one, she recalled with delight.

"Mrs. Wade, please follow me." A voice interrupted her thoughts.

Penny got to her feet and tried to be as solemn as this occasion called for. Her heels clacked against the cement, and the sound echoed off the walls in a jarring reminder of where she was.

She stepped into the next room and heard the door clang shut behind her. After taking her seat, she peered through the wire mesh screen and spoke. "Hello, Ellen," she said, "how are you?"

David adjusted the seat for the long drive back to Oakdale. When he had first started coming here, it had been unpleasant, to say the least. But gradually it had become a ritual he'd looked forward to with pleasure, oddly enough. His life had taken so many twists and turns lately, and this latest direction was more intriguing than anything had been for years.

It certainly hadn't started out that way. He'd begun visiting Ellen first out of curiosity, as distasteful as that was to admit. He couldn't understand how a woman he thought he knew completely could be capable of so brutal a crime. After their first few meetings, he was puzzled that prison hadn't hardened her. On the outside, she was still the same woman he loved and respected. As for her so-called crime, perhaps he had always believed deep down that it was an accident as she had claimed. But after Frannie's death, his shock had been so extreme that he had been unable to believe in her innocence.

And the evidence had been so irrefutable. He himself had been forced to admit that the level of tension between Ellen and Frannie was near the breaking point before her death. Frannie's competence as a housekeeper and a nursemaid for the children had always been unquestioned, whereas Ellen's past was shady at best. So when Ellen was first imprisoned, though he often visited her, he still couldn't believe wholeheartedly in her innocence.

Lately he'd begun to to realize that if everything that fateful night had happened just the way Ellen had claimed it had, then her behavior in prison was understandable. Nothing about her conduct seemed to suggest guilt in any way. This was why she seemed to be the same woman she had been before Frannie's death. She was the same. She hadn't killed anyone—she had simply been caught in an incredibly unfortunate circumstance for which he was fully as guilty as she. If he'd kept his eyes open, perhaps he would have seen what Frannie Brennan had been up to, and he would have prevented it.

But all this was hindsight. Though he now believed in Ellen's innocence, in the eyes of the law it remained unproven. Now he had a job to do—to uncover some kind of evidence that would vindicate Ellen and return to him his wife-to-be and the mother of his youngest son. It was all so clear to him now. Why on earth had it taken him so many months to face the truth? He decided to make up for his lack of insight and faith right then and there.

He braked the car sharply and turned into a gas station, made a U-turn around the pumps and the startled attendant, and headed back for the prison. Ellen deserved to know about this right now.

"I promised myself I wouldn't go on and on about Neil, but I just can't stop myself," Penny confessed.

"It's all right, really it is," Ellen reassured her. "Just because I'm in here doesn't mean that the rest of the world stops living."

"I know, but you've suffered so much lately. It doesn't seem fair that I should be enjoying all of this happiness, while you're . . ." She stopped, unable to find the words she wanted.

"In da stir?" Ellen rasped. "Up da river?"

"I suppose if you can have a sense of humor

about it, then so can I. It's just so hard seeing you like this, and knowing that you couldn't possibly have done what they said you did. Do you remember when we were giggling teenagers, talking about boys and life and what we wanted to be when we grew up? Not in our wildest dreams did we imagine anything like this."

"Not in our wildest nightmares, " Ellen corrected. "Me, a jailbird. Who ever would have predicted it? They certainly didn't write that in our high school yearbook—Ellen Lowell, Class Con."

Penny gazed at her friend with admiration. "If this had happened to me, I'd fall apart, I just know it. You refuse to let this get you down and you never lose hope. You're so strong, Ellen."

"Do you know what? The fact is, I'm tired of being strong, I'm tired of making the jokes, I'm tired of putting on a bright face. I just want to stop thinking about it for a little while. So please tell me about Neil. Tell me how disgustingly happy you are. I want to know, really I do."

"Well, now that we have the store on its feet, things are pretty smooth for us. I can't wait until you can visit the Wade Bookshop, Ellen. We got our hands on a great location, and business is off to a good start. You know, when Neil first suggested bookselling, I was a little scared. His decision seemed to come out of nowhere, and even to this day he's never explained it to me. But once I saw how well he took to being a bookstore proprietor, I had to admit that maybe his judgment was right. He has a knack for it, and he's so good with people that already we have a number of regular customers. The shop is going to be a success, I can tell. It's come such a long way in such a short time, kind of like me. Both the shop and I have the same person to thank, too. It's been Neil for both of us. Ellen, I just can't wait—maybe I shouldn't say this—but I can't wait for you to get out of here. Neil is such a fine man, and I know you'd like each other. I don't think I've ever met anyone kinder or gentler or more straightforward. He's so honest sometimes it hurts, and I love him for it."

Penny paused to reflect. "When we were kids, Ellen, do you remember? You were always the conservative one, and I was the little rebel, never quite doing what I was told. And now look at us. I'm here telling you how happy I am with security and stability, and you . . . Well, you're standing up to the entire judicial system of the state. Even the outcome of the trial didn't shake your faith in yourself, and I know I could never be that strong. When Jeff was on trial, I tried so hard to believe in him, but eventually I got worn down, and right before they brought in the verdict, I was ready to send him to the elec—" She broke off in mid-word. "Oh, Ellen, I'm sorry. I guess I'm pretty stupid sometimes."

Ellen's eyes filled up with tears. "Everyone says I'm such a survivor and I guess I am, Penny. But sometimes I think I'd be better off if I'd gotten the death penalty. Do you want to know something I've never told anyone? Each day I have to force my eyes open because I don't want to look at those bars one more time. And the only thing that ever makes me get out of bed is the thought that one day maybe I'll be back with Danny. He's all I have left that means anything to me anymore."

"But what about David? Doesn't he visit you nearly every day?" Penny was surprised to hear Ellen speak this way. The last she had heard, David was staunchly supporting Ellen as well as doing his best to keep her up to date on how the boys were getting along.

"Oh, he makes an appearance all right. But I can't really say that I enjoy his company any more. I don't want him to stand by me out of some sense of duty or something—I want him to stand by me because he believes in me!" She gripped the edge of the metal table that separated her from her friend and leaned up so that her face nearly touched the screen. "I'm not guilty of Frannie Brennan's murder! It was an accident. She fell as she was coming after me, and I was an innocent victim. I want the man who loves me to accept my innocence without question. David doesn't. Somewhere inside himself he harbors doubts, but he hides them from me. I've tried to get him to face it, but he won't, and now I feel it's no use. I've made up my mind. I'm going to ask him not to come here any more. It's just too painful for me."

"That's a little harsh, don't you think?" Penny hated to see her friend in such distress, but she didn't want her to cast away the one person who really cared about her.

"How would you know?" Ellen snapped. "You've gone on and on about how honest and sensitive your Neil is. How do you suppose I like having a man who not only doesn't trust me, but also doesn't even have the strength of character to admit it?"

"I know you're very hurt, and when you're hurt, you lash out at those who love you the most. I know because I've done the same thing. But it doesn't get you anything but more pain, Ellen, and you've had enough of that to last yourself a lifetime. Give him a chance and give yourself a chance. Please."

Ellen weakened slightly. She stared at her hands, sighed, then took a deep breath. "I've had to be strong for myself for so long, and I'm sick of it. I guess I just don't want to tolerate anyone who doesn't give me one hundred per cent."

Just then the matron stepped forward. "Excuse me, Mrs. Wade, but I'm afraid your visit is over. It's time for Miss Lowell to return to her cell."

Penny stood up reluctantly, then bent down for one final request. "I beg you, Ellen, think about what I said. It's important. And I'll see you soon."

"Goodbye," Ellen said, "and thank you for coming. Your visits . . . they mean a lot to me, even if I don't show it." She drew herself up and smiled bravely.

"Wait! Let me through!" a voice shouted from the next room, as a loud commotion broke out. "I've got to see her. It's important." Penny and Ellen gasped in unison as David rushed through the door, with two guards at his heels. One of them tried to grab him, but he shook them off. "This will only take a minute," he said firmly, "so let me speak."

The guards backed off as David ran forward. "I've been a fool, Ellen. I love you and I always have. But I've never known how to talk to you here. I can never manage to say the right things."

You're doing fine, just keep going, Penny encouraged silently. Ellen was obviously moved, but she kept her position away from her seat.

"Please hear me out," David begged fervently. "I believe in you. I know you didn't kill Frannie, and I guess I've always known it. I never ever thought you were guilty—but I hesitated to commit myself to your innocence. I just let the lack of proof scare me off. Please forgive me."

Slowly Ellen walked toward him, and as if they were mirror images of each other, together they sank into the chairs on opposite sides of the barrier. David raised his hands to the screen, and moments later, Ellen did the same. Through the mesh, their fingertips met in a wordless token of their feeling for each other.

Penny smiled with satisfaction and tiptoed from the room.

"Welcome to the Wade Bookshop," Neil called out heartily. "I'll be with you in just a minute." He set down the stack of mysteries which had just come in and walked to the front of the store. "Is there something in particular I could help you with today?"

"Yes, actually there is. My daughter has just married a wonderful man, and I'm worried she isn't taking care of him properly. Have you a cookbook you could recommend?"

"Oh, Mother Hughes," Neil laughed lightly. "I didn't recognize you from the back. What a lovely surprise. To what do I owe the honor?"

"Well, as delightful as it is to see you," Nancy teased, "I was actually looking for Penny. Is she here?"

"Not yet, but she should be back soon. She went to see Ellen, but I'm sure she intended to return before closing. Can you stay a while or are you your usual busy self?"

"I'd love to have a chat, dear, but I have some errands to run that I was hoping she could help me with. Then I'm meeting your father-in-law. We're having a date tonight." She giggled. "He's taking me to the movies."

"Then as much as I would love to, I won't keep you. Give my best to Dad, will you?" Neil took her by the arm and escorted her to the door.

"Goodbye, dear," Nancy said as she hurried down the steps to the sidewalk. "Tell Penny I was here, and give her my love."

Neil waved cheerfully, praying that he hadn't given away his uneasiness. That had been a close call, but if he could fool sharp-eyed Nancy Hughes, then he could deceive just about anyone.

He didn't enjoy his deceit, but to him it seemed like a necessary evil. After all that Penny had been through, she deserved her time of happiness, and he would do anything to prolong it as much as he could. But it wasn't completely in his control.

Back when he'd been forced to give up his medical practice, his condition had been far less severe than it was now. That was when the lies had started, and they had grown dramatically since then. It was getting harder and harder to cover up—he knew that. At the point where he couldn't recognize his own mother-in-law, he knew he couldn't keep hiding the problem. Soon he would have to admit it openly. The plain, simple truth was that Neil Wade was going blind.

As soon as his illness had been diagnosed, he had given up surgery. Shortly after that he had dropped medicine entirely, telling Penny he needed a change. Something less stressful, he'd said, like a bookstore, and they had opened this shop soon afterwards. Its warmth and friendliness attracted customers from all over Oakdale, and its cheerfulness gave Neil comfort and solace.

His eyesight had even stopped deteriorating for a while, but now it seemed the remission was over. His doctors had warned him that the progress of his loss wouldn't be steady, that there might be long periods where he would even seem to gain his vision back. But the eventual result would be total, permanent blindness, and this was what frightened him the most. How could he do this to Penny? She had finally recovered from a series of catastrophes, and soon she would be caring for an invalid husband. He owed it to her to protect her from this awful future as long as he could.

But now his game would soon be over. Mrs. Hughes hadn't picked up on his lapse this time, but next time he might not be so lucky. With a heavy heart he sat on the stool near the register and thought about what he would do. Eventually he would have to break the news to Penny, but he wanted to put that off as long as possible. He had taken his deceit this far, and there was really nothing to be gained by giving it up now. A lie was a lie, no matter how you looked at it, and it would be no more acceptable just because it didn't go on quite so long.

Still time was running out. His doctors had told him that vision in the middle distance would fade first, especially under weak light, and that was exactly what had happened today with Penny's mother. When he had peered up toward the front of the store, he could only make out a vague dark shape. Even when he had stood in front of her, he hadn't been sure of her identity. He hadn't realized who she was until she spoke.

Perhaps a return visit to the eye institute was in order, but how could he accomplish this without alerting Penny? Ideally he would wait until he could send her to Chicago on some sort of book buying pretext, but there wasn't time for that. What he should do is phone for an appointment, and then deal with getting her out of the way later. As for the phone call, there was no time like the present, since she was still out visiting Ellen.

He'd just picked up the phone and started to dial it when the door opened. A shadowy figure walked in, and fearing it might be his wife, he hung up hastily.

"Hello," he called out noncommitally, busying himself with a pile of books on the desk. Surreptitiously, he glanced up to see a shape much like Penny's. "Is that you, dear?"

"Is that who?" asked a voice he'd never heard before. "I just came in for a copy of the latest Perry Mason. Do you have it?"

Chapter Eleven
A Tragic Discovery

Nancy stood in the doorway of Donald's room. "You know," she said wistfully, "nothing breaks a mother's heart quite like seeing her oldest son packing."

"Mother, I'm an adult. Didn't it ever occur to you that I would move out one day?" Don tossed a pile of shirts into the suitcase which lay open on his bed.

"Dear me," Nancy said, sighing. "I don't know which is more distressing, watching you leave home or watching how you pack. Here, let me help you."

Don continued his work. "You don't need to, Mom. I know you don't approve of what I'm doing, and you really don't need to contribute to my downfall."

"Donald!" Nancy shot back. "I apologized once already for that unfortunate choice of words, and I don't deserve to be reminded. I was angry and upset, but I don't suppose you can understand that. When you have children of your own—"

"Really, Mother, let's not start again. I'm moving out and that's that. I still love you and I agree I should accept your apology and forget about it." He straightened up and gave her a reassuring hug. "For the first time in my life, I'm making a decision on my own, and I feel good about it. Please don't spoil it for me."

"That's the last thing I want to do," Nancy protested. "But your father and I . . ." Her voice trailed off, and she sat on the bed next to the suitcase and looked at her son for a full minute. "You're right," she agreed. "This is your life and you're in charge of it. I have no right to meddle. Now give me those clothes and let me show you how to pack properly."

Penny skittered along the sidewalk, her feet barely touching the cement. She drank in the afternoon sunshine and drew in air in deep, heady gulps. It had been years since she had felt spring fever as overpowering as this. And it had lasted so long. Even Neil was getting tired of her constant good humor, and she supposed he was right. It could become irritating. It certainly had been an inappropriate mood for her to visit with Ellen last week.

But it felt so good. Last spring had come so soon after Jeff's death that she'd barely noticed the change of seasons. But this year, she was so eager to break out of the winter doldrums that she'd begun her spring housecleaning before Ground Hog Day.

So many things were going right for her now,

and she was finally mature enough to appreciate what fulfillment life with Neil could bring her. If only he could share her joy! He seemed so moody lately, and that was the main reason she had left the shop early that day. No matter what she said or did, it seemed to rub him the wrong way, and so she had decided that she would walk over to her mother's house to pay her a visit.

Neil had suggested, rather actually insisted, that she take the car and then come back for him at the end of the day, but she had refused. It was such a lovely afternoon that she preferred to walk along the tree-shaded streets in the neighborhood in which she had grown up, she told him, and he could pick her up at the Hughes' house before dinner. Then she had flown out of the shop before he had a chance to reply.

Forgetting Neil's current mood, she was still the luckiest person she knew. She was married to a man she loved deeply—she was satisfied with her life. Before the wedding they had discussed adopting children, and Neil seemed as excited at the prospect as Penny had been. But they had both resolved that starting a family would wait until they were well past the initial honeymoon stage. Their marriage was a very happy one, even though they'd been married a very short time. They'd matured as a couple in ways that she and Jeff had not even begun to after several stormy years of courtship and one year of marriage.

But when she'd broached the idea of adoption the other evening, Neil hadn't seemed too happy about it. He had tried to cover his reluctance, but it was obvious. So Penny had agreed to table the discussion for a while, but she warned him that she didn't intend to wait long.

This was a minor problem compared to what some of her friends and family members were going through, she admitted. She paused at a picket fence to admire a grouping of jonquils. The sweet fragrance of the soft yellow flowers drifted up and gave her a giddy sense of abandon. If nature could make such intoxicating scents, she thought, and just waft them into the air, then she certainly could use her wonderful gifts of sensitivity and understanding, distributing them among those she loved.

The first person to benefit from her humanity would have to be poor Ellen, though it was hard to think of her as poor. Despite years of trouble, capped by the nightmarish accident that sent her to jail, Ellen hung onto her belief in herself with total conviction. But she needed support. Her prison term wasn't likely to be reduced for quite some time yet. As a matter of fact, Ellen had mentioned that parole was years away. Perhaps there were ways in which Penny could help with the boys, especially Danny, who was having a very hard time adjusting to Ellen's absence, coming as it did so soon after Betty's death.

If only Penny could uncover facts that would lead to Ellen's release. She believed totally in Ellen's innocence, even though there wasn't a shred of hard evidence to back her up. Often she dreamed of finding a new undiscovered witness, though she knew that was just a fantasy. Still there were things she could do to make Ellen happier, and she was determined to do them.

That left the problem of Donald. Now there

was a problem without a solution. His latest move seemed to be a reaction to what had happened in the past rather than what he really wanted. She wished she could reach him, but all her efforts to communicate hadn't worked. And soon it would be too late.

When Don had first announced his plans, Nancy and Chris were beside themselves. They had always wanted him to get married and settle down, but Janice Turner had never been someone they could approve of. In fact, they had succeeded in breaking up the relationship once before, and Janice had moved to California. When they'd heard that she'd found a husband, they'd breathed sighs of relief.

But now she was back in Oakdale as a widow with two daughters to support, and she wanted to take up with Don where she had left off. She accomplished this neatly, partly because of his heartbreak over Ellen. Her brother was always so vulnerable where women were concerned, Penny thought. He'd made so many mistakes because he needed female attention so much. Some men were blinded by love itself, but Donald was blinded by the need for love.

Janice had recognized this quality in Donald and was now capitalizing on it. He had proposed already, and if they followed through with their plans, soon they'd be married. Furthermore, Janice wanted to move back to California, and Donald didn't object.

As devastated as she was by the situation, Nancy could do nothing, and neither could Penny. Chris just stayed out of it, except for occasional advice. Eventually Penny and her mother accepted the inevitable and gave Donald their blessing. At last everyone in the Hughes' household realized that Donald had the right to make his own mistakes. This he was doing with a vengeance.

If only, Penny kept thinking. If only. If only he had never met Janice. If only Ellen had returned his love. If only he had met someone else before Janice came back into his life. And now if only he would listen to what she had to say. She promised herself she would give it one last try.

She stepped up her pace and hurried along to her parents' house. She knew Donald would probably be there, and if she could just get him alone, maybe she could talk some sense into him. She turned the corner onto that familiar street and could see Donald's car in the driveway at the end of the block. Good, he's still home, she exulted. It's not too late.

Just then he emerged from the front door with a suitcase in his hand and his coat over his arm. He opened the trunk and wedged the suitcase in between several other pieces of luggage.

"Donald," Penny called, but he hopped into the front seat without a backwards glance.

"Don! Wait!" she yelled, expecting him at least to roll down the window and speak to her. Instead he put the car in gear, backed out of the driveway, and drove off in the opposite direction without so much as a goodbye wave to his sister.

Penny stood on the sidewalk and watched until he was out of sight. The last few steps home were as long to her as any journey she had taken. If only, she chided herself as she turned up the driveway. If only.

She banged the screen door in frustration. "What is wrong with that brother of mine?" she called out to no one in particular.

"I'm afraid it's my fault," her mother answered. She was sitting at the kitchen table distractedly leafing through a cookbook. "I promised him I would mind my own business and I guess I didn't quite do that. Donald was doing some packing in preparation for the big move out West, and everything was going along all right until I opened my mouth one too many times. One thing led to another, and I ended up telling him that if he was so anxious for his freedom from his family that he should just take his luggage and move into a hotel until after the ceremony, and then he could do as he wished. I've never spoken to him like that."

Penny pulled up a chair and sat down beside her. "Mom, you did the best you could. We all did. Remember, we agreed it was time for him to grow up, and I guess this is just part of the process. It must be hard to let your children do things you know will hurt them, but you have to allow them their independence. How else do people learn, if not from their own mistakes? You and Dad let me make a fool out of myself more than once—now please give your son the same privilege."

Nancy looked at her daughter with admiration. "I suppose I should listen to you. After all, you've gotten your life back on track, so you must have learned something."

"I admit, I don't think my life has ever been more wonderful, at least not recently. Meeting Neil was just about the luckiest thing that could have happened to me, and thank heavens I was ready to accept what he could offer me. These last few months have been indescribable, Mom. I feel a peace, a security I've never experienced before. I just know that everything's going to work out for us. Neil's so steady, so reliable, and I love him so much for that. I can't think of anything that could come up that Neil wouldn't be able to handle, and that's very comforting."

"After what you've been through, dear, you deserve whatever you can get," Nancy said as she got up to answer the telephone.

"Hello," she said into the mouthpiece. "Well, were your ears burning?"

Penny jumped up. "Let me talk to him, Mom."

"You what?" Nancy exclaimed as she motioned Penny away. "Of course, dear, I'll tell her. Don't you worry about a thing. I'll handle it. Goodbye."

"What's wrong?" Penny inquired worriedly.

Nancy put her finger over the button and dialed. "Nothing. Neil just can't find the car keys. He asked me to tell you, and to ask your father if he would stop on the way home from the office and give him a lift over here."

"It was a lovely meal, and so nice of your parents to go to so much trouble for us. I feel like such a fool losing the keys. I just don't know what's wrong with me lately." Neil flicked on the lamp next to the bed and sat down and pulled off his shoes.

Penny looked at him with concern. "I don't know what's wrong with you either, Neil, but it has me a little worried. Is there something you're not telling me?"

"Whatever would make you ask that?" he countered.

"Obviously there's something wrong, Neil Wade, or you'd never avoid a simple question like that. Now what do I have to do to drag it out of you?"

Neil went into the bathroom and laboriously spread toothpaste on his toothbrush, deftly keeping his hands out of Penny's view. "There's nothing wrong. How many times do I have to repeat it?"

"Until I believe you, dear, and I don't yet. You know, the longer you keep this from me, the more convinced I become that it's something serious. So you'd better level with me before I start to get frantic." Penny tried to keep her tone light, but she had a sinking feeling that whatever Neil was hiding was a bigger problem than she'd ever imagined. "Now come in here and talk to me. I want some answers right now."

"There's nothing to tell, so you might as well stop worrying," Neil insisted as he closed the bathroom door and made for the bed. Suddenly he stumbled and fell across the bedside table, knocking the lamp to the floor.

Penny gasped and rushed to his side. "Are you all right?"

"I'm fine. I just tripped on the rug. Pick up the lamp for me, will you? I seem to be awfully clumsy lately," he said as he straightened up the table and climbed into bed.

"Neil, there's something terribly wrong, and you must tell me. You've had a lot of these little accidents lately, and something tells me there's more to it than you're letting on. Now what is it?"

Neil stared off into space, gathering up his courage for what he knew must come. The silence felt deafening to Penny, but she waited patiently, summoning all her strength to keep her fear in check. Finally Neil turned to her and took her hand.

"You must promise me," he began, his voice thick with emotion, "that you'll listen until I'm completely done with my story, and then we'll decide together how to handle it."

"I promise," she said, mystified by his sudden change.

"It goes back a long way, back to when we first met. I was still in medicine then and hoped to continue building up my practice here in Oakdale. I was putting in long hours and even taking research material home with me at night, so when I first noticed the problem, I put it down to simple overwork. But it got worse, and finally I could ignore it no longer, so I went to a specialist in Chicago. He examined me and gave me his diagnosis. I won't bore you with the name or the medical details, but quite simply I'm going blind. It's irreversible. That's why I'm losing things or bumping into things. I can't see them anymore. I'm so sorry, Penny . . . oh, my little Penny . . ." He choked up and put his arms around her and began to sob.

In shock, she could think of nothing rational to say. She knew that being a doctor himself, he would have investigated every possible recourse. There was only one thing she could do. She must accept this as soon as she could and then she must devote her time and energy to caring for him. But it was too early to think about any of that now.

"Neil," she said softly as she stroked his hair, "I love you. Nothing will ever change that."

Penny fell into a light, fitful sleep. This changes everything, she thought just as she drifted off, but she was too exhausted to think of exactly how her plans would be altered. Dimly she perceived one very precious desire slipping from her, but she didn't have the courage to bring it closer to her consciousness. She would do that in the morning in the clear light of day.

Late that night, she awoke from a dream she could not recall, but she knew it had something to do with babies. Babies that she could once have had, but now never would.

Chapter Twelve
New Hope, New Despair

A lone crimson leaf fluttered down past the picture window and landed on the grass next to the hydrangea bush. Ellen watched in fascination. For so long her only view of the outside world had been through bars that now she revelled in each and every sight that Mother Nature brought to her.

But by far the most precious sight she could see was that of David and the two boys raking up leaves on the front lawn. Actually, David was doing most of the raking, and the boys, Danny particularly, were tumbling in the pile of leaves, scattering them almost as fast as their father could gather them up. Finally he gave in to their horseplay and tossed the rake aside. He picked up Danny and held him aloft as Paul threw a clump of leaves over them both.

Ellen loved Saturdays. On this day more than any other day of the week, she felt the unity of the family around her and she knew she was where she belonged at last.

She turned back to her visitor. "I'm sorry, Penny. I wasn't listening to one single word you said. Please forgive me. Sometimes I get so caught up in what's happening around me that I can't concentrate on a simple conversation. I'm not used to all this stimulation. Life 'in the slammer' can be pretty dull."

Penny laughed. "You know, there were so many times over the last year that I thought of you and how you had such courage and faith. And I said to myself, I can get through this. It's nothing compared to what my friend Ellen Lowell is going through."

"It's Ellen Stewart now, I'd like to remind you," she said, laughing. "I am Mrs. Dr. David Stewart. That's how you say it, isn't it?"

"It doesn't matter how you say it—it's still pretty unbelievable, don't you think? One minute you're in the slammer, as you so delicately refer to it, and the next minute you're walking down the aisle. Please tell me again how David managed it." Penny poured herself another cup of coffee from the carafe on the table.

"Once that husband of mine sets his mind on something, he doesn't give up until he accomplishes it. First he looked everywhere for witnesses, but of course all he could dig up were people who'd heard us arguing at the playground, and that didn't do me any good at all. Then he went around the neighborhood trying to find someone who could refute what the people next door had said. Again he met with a dead end. Desperately, he started looking into Frannie's background, and that's when he hit pay dirt."

"I just adore your colorful language, Ellen. Did you learn that when you were 'sent up the river'?" Penny snickered, but as Ellen shot her a sidelong glance, she covered herself hastily. "But go ahead. I didn't mean to interrupt."

"So when David started nosing around in Frannie's past, that's where he came across Scratchy Malloy."

Penny laughed. "Scratchy Malloy? Ellen, you're making this up."

"Thank heavens I'm not," her friend retorted, "or I wouldn't be here to tell you this heartrending story that's amusing you so much. This Malloy character was Frannie's half-brother and had worked with her for a family out in Minnesota. He had been the handyman, and Frannie had been the housekeeper, nursemaid, and whatever, pretty much like she was here. Well, apparently it didn't take long for Frannie to decide that she wanted to be much more than an employee, so she set about making that a reality. Fortunately her schemes were uncovered, and they let her go before she was able to do any real damage."

"Is that when she came here to Oakdale?"

"Yes. She left her past completely behind her and evidently didn't mention it at all when she applied for the position with David and Betty. But the thing was, she continued to keep in touch with her half-brother, and that's what eventually led to my release. She'd written him a letter telling him about David and how he was her chance for a better life, and the only thing standing in her way was me. She'd stop at nothing to get rid of me, she told him, and luckily for me, he'd saved the letter. When David first found him he refused even to admit he'd ever heard of Frannie, but when David told him what was at stake, he broke down and told the whole story. From there on, it was easy. David and my lawyer went to the judge and before I even knew what was going on, I was out of jail. And here I am."

Penny leaned back on the cushions. "You know," she said. "we're a couple of very lucky ladies. Not too many people would think so, but we both have discovered something very valuable."

"And what is that, may I ask?"

"I wish I knew. But after all this suffering, we must have learned something. Now if we could just figure out what it is." For the first time in her life, Penny was comfortable making light of her problems. Finally she had reached the point where Neil's blindness was no longer a matter of life and death. True, she was desperately unhappy at having to put off considering adopting a child, but her husband's needs came first.

"That reminds me. How's everything with Neil? Is there anything new?" Ellen hated to bring up such a painful topic, since there was never any progress to report.

"Actually, he's going in for some tests today. I'm not getting my hopes up because I've been through this so many times before. But the doctor did say that certain types of his illness were responding to some new treatment they've discovered. Neil said he'd call me after he went to the doctor's office. That's why I'm out visiting today. I want to keep my mind off it. Just knowing that the doctor is taking time to see him on a Saturday makes me nervous."

"I had no idea. This must be very difficult for you, Penny. Is there anything I can do?"

Penny sipped her coffee. "No," she said, "except maybe pray for Neil. I love him no matter what, but the truth is, he deserves better than this. He's a fine man, so intelligent and so interested in the world around him,—it just isn't fair that his sight is being taken from him." She sighed. "If only he'd complain about the injustice of it all, but he never does. He just accepts it without a murmur, yet he's ready every time they want to try something different. Sometimes I think he feels like a guinea pig, but he still goes through with it. The other day he said that it was terrible going in for these tests and desperately wishing they'd find a cure, then each time having the same result"

Ellen was silent for a few minutes. Then she said, "I wish you both all the best, Penny, you know I do, and so does David. We both feel so helpless, though. It's hard to see your friends suffer. You must know how that feels," Ellen told her slowly, comfortingly. "All the philosophizing in the world can't lessen the pain of seeing your loved ones go through such terrible ordeals."

"The worst part is, I just can't stop myself from thinking that maybe this time they'll find a way to keep Neil from losing his sight." Now Penny started to cry. "I try so hard to stay hopeful, but not to expect too much, and I just don't know how much longer I can hang on. Each day Neil's vision gets weaker and weaker, and of course he hates to ask me to do anything for him. I already do the driving and everything around the house. But the really agonizing part is covering up for him at the bookstore. He still likes to believe that he can handle the work there without making lots of mistakes, but he can't. I always have to make some excuse to stay late so that I can check the shelves or go over the accounts to see what he's missed. I can't stand keeping anything from him, but I can't take away what self-respect he has left—I can't tell him he isn't able to work anymore. Oh, Penny, where will it all end?"

Neil left the doctor's office in a hurry, trying to hide his elation. For the first time since he started going to the institute for tests, he was permitting himself some hope. He had performed so well on this battery of tests that the doctor had called up the eye institute in Chicago and made an appointment for Neil to see them next week. Once they'd seen Neil's results, they'd insisted on seeing him as soon as possible. A new form of surgery had proven successful in a case like Neil's and they were eager to examine him to determine his eligibility for a similar operation.

Perhaps his months of semi-darkness were soon to be over. He grasped the bannister and made his way down the stairs. Dear God, he prayed, please let this end. Please let Penny and me be released from this bondage.

He pushed through the door and felt the welcome rays of sunshine hit his face as he stepped out onto the sidewalk. It was certainly easier for him to see in bright light than it was indoors, although any sort of reflection was almost painfully brilliant. He squinted and shaded his eyes, peering down the street to plot the path ahead of him. Walking into pedestrians was always embarrassing, since his impaired vision wasn't immediately noticeable to passers-by.

Soon all these difficulties would be behind him—he just knew it. He walked faster in anticipation. He didn't know how he would contain himself until next week. His only regret was that Penny wasn't here to share this special moment with him. He had wanted to visit the doctor alone, fully expecting that the outcome would be as gloomy as ever. There was a phone booth in the drugstore on the next corner, he remembered, and he began to plan exactly how he'd break the news to her.

So many things would change. He could become a full working partner in the bookstore again, and he wouldn't have to wait at home in the evenings while his wife corrected the mistakes he had made during the daytime. Instead of being dependent on Penny, he could begin to give her the kind of support she deserved. Together they could work out everything.

Even more important, he could tell her that he was ready to become a father, and they could begin their search for a child immediately. This news would bring Penny the happiness she so richly deserved. It had been such a hard road for her, but she'd taken on the burden of his blindness without any complaint. She'd had to accept the fact that she'd never become even an adoptive mother and that must have taken reserves of strength he'd never known she had. But now all of that was behind them. How thrilled she would be to hear it!

He stopped at the crosswalk and waited for the light to change. He held up his hand to shade his sensitive eyes from the glare, so that he'd be able to tell immediately when it was safe for him to step into the street. He was about to start on a whole new life and couldn't wait to begin.

"I know I shouldn't do this, but I'm going to anyway. Do you think I'm wrong?" Penny turned to Ellen for support.

"No, I don't think you're wrong to want to know what happened at the doctor's office. But I think you should wait a few minutes and talk to Neil instead of calling the doctor yourself." Ellen had stacked the coffee cups on the tray and was passing by the telephone on the way to the kitchen.

"I just can't wait any more. Suddenly something tells me that there's good news," Penny tossed over her shoulder as she swiftly leafed through the directory. "Ah, here it is. I hope Neil is still there."

"Best of luck," Ellen called from the sink. "I hope you get some good news."

Penny held the receiver close. "Hello? This is Penny Wade, and I'm looking for my husband. Is he there?" She listened for a moment. "Oh, he did? Thank you. I'll try him back at the shop in a few minutes. Can you tell me—was there anything special to report? Did the doctor complete the examination all right?"

Within seconds she broke out with a sparkling grin. "Ellen! Come here. Quick!" She held the receiver away from her mouth briefly, then spoke. "Yes, doctor. The nurse just told me a little bit. What did you find out?"

By then Ellen was at her side. Penny nodded intently several times, then drew in her breath excitedly. "Thank you so much. I understand this isn't a cure, I promise I do, but you must realize it's simply the only good news we've had for quite some time. Thank you again." Impulsively she threw her arms around Ellen and hugged her.

"What? Tell me, please."

"Well," she began slowly, "it's nothing conclusive of course, and he said we mustn't plan anything, but in some cases like Neil's, they have found that a new procedure has been effective. Neil goes to Chicago next week to undergo more tests to determine whether or not the operation could be successful." Penny grabbed her coat off the hall chair and made for the door. "If anyone calls for me, especially Neil, I'll be at the bookstore in just a few minutes."

There we go, Neil thought. The traffic light flickered, and he decided it was safe to move into the street. He chuckled, telling himself that he could forget about having to carry a white cane to mark himself as legally blind. It would not be necessary. Before his sight deteriorated to the point where he absolutely couldn't get along without one, he would have been to Chicago and had the operation. Why me? he asked delightedly. Dear God, why me? The heavens were indeed smiling upon him, and he was eternally thankful. He stepped forward.

He was so caught up with his newfound optimism that he didn't hear the shouts of the other pedestrians. He didn't hear the honk of the horn or the screech of the brakes.

When they reached him moments later, he was lying in a crumpled heap at the side of a floral delivery truck. The side door had popped open in the panic stop, and mangled bouquets lay scattered on the pavement, surrounding the inert form.

In shock, the driver still sat behind the steering wheel. Then he leaped out and stood beside Neil's body. "He just walked right in front of me. He never even looked," he moaned. "What is he, blind or something?"

Nancy Hughes shut off the iron and propped it up carefully, then with several hangers full of freshly pressed shirts in her hand, she walked to the phone.

"Hello," she said distractedly. "No, this is her mother. I really don't know where she is at the moment. You should try the Wade Book Shop in the center of town. Perhaps her husband can help you locate her." She was about to put down the phone, but the urgency of the caller's voice prompted her to ask, "Is there something wrong?"

Chapter Thirteen
New Hope, New Life

Penny rested her hand on the mantelpiece and gazed at the brightly decorated tree. "You know, Mom, you were right. Not having a tree would have been wrong. It does make me feel better, and it helps me put things in perspective."

"What was that, dear? I can't hear you," Nancy called from the kitchen. "Why don't you come in and join us? I'll fix you some breakfast."

"Just don't ask for toast." That was Chris, and Penny reached the doorway just in time to see her father wipe a blackened crumb from his lips.

"Very funny, dear," Nancy retorted as she sideswiped him with a dish towel. "Just this once I didn't get it quite right."

"Perhaps I should have gotten you a new toaster for Christmas," her husband continued. "Would that have helped?"

"I'm sure I have an extra one packed away in the garage," Penny chimed in, "from either my first marriage or my second."

"You're awfully chipper this morning," Nancy remarked, "and I'm glad to see it. Is there some secret to your happiness that you'd like to let us in on?"

Penny plopped herself down at the table. "As a matter of fact, there is, only I won't discuss it until you've made me two scrambled eggs," she said as she shot a glance at her father, "and don't forget the toast."

Nancy shut the refrigerator door. "This sounds pretty mysterious. Can't you give a mother a hint?"

"I'll tell you all about it. Just be patient. I guess I should have expected a cross-examination, what with being the only Hughes child in the house." Penny turned her nose up in mock annoyance, then winked at her father.

"I'm getting curious too, sweetheart, I must admit. And you're right, what with Donald in California, Susan at her friend's house for a few days, and Bob out doing something or other, your poor old folks don't have anyone to worry about but you. Even Grandpa's away visiting Edith for the holidays, so you have our undivided attention."

Chris took his daughters' hand. Though he was pleased to see that she was recovering from the trauma of Neil's unfortunate death, he still kept a watchful eye on her moods. She'd been through so much in her young life that he was amazed she was able to have any kind of hope at all. Yet she appeared to be doing just that. Her first step had been to put the past firmly behind her, which ironically enough gave her the freedom to bring it up for discussion anytime she pleased. Only since Neil had been killed was she even able to mention Jeff's accident without threatening to go to pieces. She now seemed able to accept the loss of both her husbands with a depth of maturity that Chris was not sure that even he had.

It was lucky, he thought, if lucky was the right word, that Neil's death had come when it had. Penny had been emotionally strong enough to weather the storm, and he and Nancy had been free of problems from their other children. They had been able to devote all their time and energy to Penny. And now a scant two months later, their eldest daughter was facing the future much older and wiser, but also with hope and promise.

"So?" he said. "We're waiting."

Penny dug into her eggs ravenously. After several bites, she said, "I've been up all night thinking about this and I've come to a decision. Do you remember when Ellen was so upset after Tim's death? She realized she had to get her life in order, so she went away for a while to think things over. And do you see how well she's doing now? So I've decided to do the same thing."

Nancy sat down immediately and leaned in to her daughter. "Why, Penny," she asked, "whatever do you mean?"

Penny looked her mother square in the eye. "I'm leaving Oakdale. I'm going to Europe and I don't know when I'll be back."

Ellen Stewart felt rotten. She tossed back the sheets in haste and stumbled into the bathroom, shutting the door behind her. She felt woozy, sick, and tired all at once. What a time to get the flu, right between the holidays. Then as mysteriously as it had come, her nausea passed. How peculiar, she thought, as she made her way back to the bed.

"David," she called as loudly as she could, but she couldn't be sure her weak voice would carry all the way downstairs. "David, when you have a minute, would you come up here?" She lay back on the pillow and closed her eyes. It couldn't be, she thought, but come to think of it, all the signs were there. And it wasn't as if she didn't know what it felt like.

"David," she said as soon as she heard his footsteps at the top of the stairs, "I think I have some news for you."

He popped his head in the door. "What kind of . . ? Ellen honey, you look awful . . . I mean, you don't look so well this morning. Is something wrong?"

"Well, maybe yes and maybe no. Either I have the most terrible case of the flu that was ever invented, and you'll have to wait on me hand and foot for the next week, or I am expecting the next little Stewart, in which case you'll have to wait on me hand and foot for the next eight months or so." She looked at him innocently. "Which would you prefer?"

David's eyes misted over. Several times he tried to speak, but couldn't. Eventually he choked out, "A baby? You're going to have a baby?"

"The last time I heard, that's what 'expecting' meant. Do you have anything to say?"

"Well, yes I do, Mrs. Stewart, yes I do," he answered smoothly. "I'm really . . . um . . . I'm so . . . er . . . I guess I'm at a loss for words. Will a kiss do?" He leaned over and softly stroked her hair, then lovingly and tenderly put his lips to her cheek. "I'm very, very happy."

Ellen ran her fingers down his arm. "This is the greatest gift I could have gotten, as if simply being here with you and Danny and Paul weren't enough. I'm so blessed this year to have my first holiday home, and now this! It's a new beginning for us, David, at the end of a year of new beginnings. Something tells me this is the most wonderful omen ever." She smiled with satisfaction, then laughed outright. "That morning so many years ago when we met at the train station, I admit I liked you, but it never occurred to me that one day I'd carry your baby. And here we are, man and wife, about to become parents. Whoever said that miracles never happen?"

"Donald, how are you? I've been waiting for your call." Nancy spoke unnaturally loudly, so as to be heard over the static. "How is everyone,—Janice, the girls? Yes, we're all fine, and we've had a lovely holiday, except of course that you weren't here with us. Penny's doing well, considering, but I'll write you all about it. It's much too long to go into over the phone. The weather here is exactly what you'd expect, and please don't tell me how pleasant it is in California. I don't want to know. All I want to know about is you. Please tell me everything you're up to."

For several minutes she listened without even so much as an mmm-hmmm. Then at last she said, "I love you too, dear, and your father and I would love to see you whenever you can make it.

Yes, dear, me too. I love you. Goodbye."

After she hung up, she sighed deeply and wiped her eyes. Being a mother could be just about the hardest job in the world. There was so much she wanted to say to her son, yet so little she could offer in the way of help without damaging their relationship. When he had married Janice, he made it perfectly clear that he wouldn't tolerate any interference from his parents, particularly his mother. Now Nancy was wary of saying anything that might be misconstrued. Yet she desperately wanted to reach out through the telephone wires and shake some sense into that boy. She could tell that he wasn't altogether happy with his marriage, yet he couldn't bring himself to change it. It was so frustrating—there was just nothing she could do! She would bide her time, that was all, she decided with reluctance. Then when he came to her for help, she would be ready.

From behind her, she heard Penny coming down the stairs. "Come sit with me in the living room," she said. "I want to talk to you."

"Good," Penny replied. "I want to talk to you too."

Nancy folded her hands in her lap. "Now I know you have your heart set on going to Europe, and I'm not going to do anything to stop you. You're a grown woman, capable of making your own choices in the world. And frankly, after all that's happened to you here, I'm not surprised you want to put some distance between you and Oakdale. I think I would too if I were in your shoes. But I'm not. I'm your mother, and there are a few things I want to say to you."

"Mom," her daughter advised, "please don't try to dampen my enthusiasm or try to talk me out of it altogether. I'm going to do it whether you want me to or not, but it would mean a great deal if you could just give me your unqualified support."

Nancy gazed at her in sudden wonder. Those words sounded so familiar, as if she had heard them once before many years ago. She probed her memory in search of a steadfast young woman who'd followed the dictates of her heart, despite the disapproval of her family. She knew this woman was very close to her, yet she couldn't pinpoint exactly who it was. Then in a flash the identity became clear to her. The young woman had been herself, about to leave home to marry a young man she had met only months before, a young man named Chris Hughes. She had loved him desperately, totally, and she knew that she must take this chance. She must leave the comfort of her home, the security of her parents' care, and all that she had ever known. She knew that if she didn't do this, she might never have another opportunity to know herself as deeply as she would in marriage with this extraordinarily fine man.

Her mother's words came to her across the years as if they had been spoken yesterday. In her mind Nancy could hear her mother's strong and clear voice as they had sat in that living room in the small farmhouse so far away and so long forgotten. "My dear, your father and I have raised you for this moment, for this time when you must leave us. And as painful as it is for me to let go of you, I know I must. Whether I think your decision is the right one isn't the issue here. The only question that matters is whether you're doing what you feel is right. It's so hard for me to keep from telling you how I feel about your leaving, but if I have any faith at all in my abilities as a mother, then I'll let you go without fear or worry. When people tell you motherhood is a thankless job, they're right in only one sense—you raise your children so that one day they can leave you. The better a mother you are, the better prepared your children are to live life without you. So go, my darling, with all my love and trust and my blessing."

Penny reached over and impulsively hugged her mother. "That was very, very beautiful," she whispered.

Through her tears Nancy realized that the strong and clear voice she had just heard had been her own. The love and understanding which she'd always longed to pass on to her children were very real. Just as she could turn to memories of her own mother for unconditional love and acceptance, so could her children remember her. As she looked at her daughter so eagerly ready for a new and exciting life, she said to herself: Nancy Hughes, you've done a good job.

SOAPS & SERIALS™—a new genre of paperback books

THE YOUNG AND THE RESTLESS
DAYS OF OUR LIVES
GUIDING LIGHT
ANOTHER WORLD
AS THE WORLD TURNS
DALLAS™
KNOTS LANDING™
CAPITOL™

Every month—a *new* book in *each* series—in your local supermarket or bookstore or in the book section of drug stores, department stores and convenience stores. Ask for **SOAPS & SERIALS**™ wherever paperback books are sold. If your local stores don't yet have **SOAPS & SERIALS**™, let us know.

For back issues of books in any of our series, write to:

SOAPS & SERIALS™
Pioneer Communications Network, Inc.
P.O. Box 5006
Rocky Hill, CT 06067

Enclose $2.50 USA/$3.25 CANADA. Add 75¢ for each book to cover shipping and handling. Please send checks or money orders only—no cash or CODs. Allow 3-4 weeks for shipment.